Psychiatric nurse Donna Callery had b... ...Mor... ...e ...t... ...he c... to g... of ... ...ancé. Her meeting with Henry Emerson, however, awakened passions which she thought long dead. Then Donna discovered why Morgan Manor was called the House of Hate. It was filled with emotions which had poisoned the minds and bodies of all its inhabitants—emotions intensified by the strange will of the late Martin Morgan who left his five daughters nothing to look forward to except the death of each other! Donna sensed this danger for herself and for her patient as well. Could she escape from the Gothic monstrosity to which she had been doomed before it was too late?

DOOMED TO HATE

Jeanne Bowman

CHIVERS LARGE PRINT
Bath, England

CURLEY LARGE PRINT
Hampton, New Hampshire

Library of Congress Cataloging-in-Publication Data

Bowman, Jeanne, 1895—
    Doomed to hate / Jeanne Bowman.
        p.   cm.
    ISBN 0–7927–1987–5 (hardcover)
    ISBN 0–7927–1986–7 (softcover)
    1. Man–woman relationships—Fiction.
2. Psychiatric nurses—Fiction.   3. Large type books.
I. Title.
[PS3503.08455D66   1994]   93–49365
813'.52—dc20   CIP

British Library Cataloguing in Publication Data available

This Large Print edition is published by Chivers Press, England, and by
Curley Large Print, an imprint of Chivers North America, 1994.

Published by arrangement with Donald MacCampbell, Inc.

U.K. Hardcover ISBN 0 7451 2229 9
U.K. Softcover   ISBN 0 7451 2240 X
U.S. Hardcover ISBN 0 7927 1987 5
U.S. Softcover   ISBN 0 7927 1986 7

© Copyright 1969, by Arcadia House

Printed in Great Britain

DOOMED TO HATE

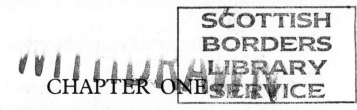

CHAPTER ONE

Dr Hal Haskell glanced at a clipboard handed him by the superintendent of nurses; barely glanced. His attention was focused on the world outside. Wonderful weather. Fishing weather. He could use a few hours loafing on the bank of a stream. Might not be a bad idea to write himself a prescription, an RX complete with hourly dosage of sunlight, the application of a shadow at proper intervals.

'You said you wanted to scan that,' Superintendent Dolores scoffed. 'Nurse left it here on her way out.'

'Yes, yes, of course.' Then he stopped and scowled. There was a movement far below in the parking area. An orderly was wheeling someone—oh, naturally, this patient and—he shook the clipboard—wheeling her out to some car. Nurse was trotting along beside.

'Dolores!' His voice rose in shock. 'You've assigned Caffery to that, er, that patient? For private home duty? Is that girl heading for the House of Hate?'

'You okayed the discharge on Montel. I know. I know she was breaking out with nerves at being held here. You believed her recovery would be quicker at—what did you call it?—the House of Hate. Not bad. I mean the term.

'Guess we've had them all in here at one time or another. Different medicos, though,' she defended herself.

'Are you intimating Nurse Caffery will not be called upon for extra services because those sisters cannot agree on who dispenses treatment? That doesn't aid your choice.'

Soberly Dolores turned. 'Doctor, Caffery is one if the best psychiatric nurses on call. I know she's young, but in this field that can be good. No crystallized formats. And, Doctor, you know the turnover in nurses we've had on other cases out there. I have a feeling she'll be able to stand up to them longer.'

'Could be.' He sighed. 'That young chap Emerson is still managing the ranch for them, isn't he? Well?'

Dolores hesitated. She could have added something more but felt she couldn't. Nor did she know she was correct in her evaluation of one Donna Maria Caffery. Time would or wouldn't tell.

She thought then of the so-called House of Hate. Hmm. Interesting. She had seen it just once, from a distance. Had she not had literally to shuffle nurses attending the five Morgan girls, whose home this was, she might have questioned Dr Haskell's terminology.

2

But they had been in one at a time, and had been discharged feeling much better than those who had attended them.

'Oh, and, Dr Haskell,' she added, she hoped, the clinching phrase, 'it takes a nurse who is young and strong to cope with the halls and stairs of that mansion. The Goths would have risen to haunt its turrets, had they known what a man named Morgan could have done with vertical lines.'

She did not add: When one is bone-weary with aching muscles, a heartache is less agonizing. In a sense this duty would give one of her favorites, Donna Maria Caffery, a rest therapy no medico could advocate.

Donna Maria Caffery, trying to catch up to the orderly, packages from the hospital pharmacy slipping from her arms, looked upon her new duty as 'just another' in a different setting.

She would be there two, three weeks, she reasoned, and went back to checking her parcels; swabs, bandages—ah, the antibiotic emollient. Now why hadn't this phlebitis Mrs Montel evidenced responded to these medications at the hospital?

True, there had been minor surgery while she was there—veins stripped and now healing. Yet in bed, with no noticeable strain, other areas were becoming activated. For some reason in view of her background, Dr Haskell had found that only discharge, a

3

return to her home, would ameliorate the condition.

And meanwhile Rose, Donna's apartment mate, would have dinners and parties, and she would not be there putting on an act of gaiety. It would be a relief to be just herself, a nurse on private duty in a big house far in the country.

She might even find relief from this hag of conscience who forever rode her shoulders. She might, or else learn to live with it.

'Yes, Mrs Montel.' Donna pushed russet brown hair to a more precise alignment. 'It is comfortable, isn't it? My one extravagance, my car. Let me test that styrofoam. It does make a soft but secure leg rest, doesn't it? Now then, ready?'

For a little while, until they were out of heavy city traffic, neither said much. But once they were on the four-lane highway, Mrs Montel spoke.

'It will be good to be home. Oh, not that I didn't enjoy the hospital, but—'

Donna let a murmur indicate interest, and her patient continued, 'So much to do this time of the year, you know. I would lie there in bed and literally set my legs to try to catch up to the duties ahead.'

And the legs, unable to respond with physical action, had swollen at the emotional urge.

'Why so much to do?' Donna asked

4

lightly.

'It's near harvest, you know. Much of the fruit, the berries and such vegetables as we preserve at the big house, are being prepared for winter use.'

Donna cast a bewildered glance. A vast ranch, the upper levels planted to grain, the lower to vegetables instantly bought up by canneries and freezing plants—and the owners of the land felt they must prepare their own?

'I didn't realize you prepared your own.' Yet wasn't Mrs Montel returning home for still another reason? The high cost of hospitalization?

'Oh, my, yes.' She sighed. 'We each like different seasonings, at times different combinations of ingredients. This way there is less criticism, silent naturally, of the one preparing a meal. Of course Hank likes everything, but after a young man has been out in the chill rain or blazing sun all day, food is food.'

Hank? Oh, yes, the stepson—or was he an adopted son?—who had signed Mrs Montel in at the hospital and fumed on hearing of her discharge.

Donna swung her car into a wide valley, breathed deeply and thought—ah, such a beautiful world. And such a foolish one. Mrs Montel's hospitalization costs would have purchased enough food for the entire family.

What a price, spending emotional pressure on one's limbs.

'You take that next turn to the right, that lane there. Our home is due west at the foot of those mountains.'

Donna took one glance at the vast pile of blue-black mountains rearing against the sky, and only training kept her from applying emotional pressure to the brakes. She could not, she would not live there even for two weeks. Not with those peaks scowling down at her, not with the memories of what one of those rugged giants had done to her life and his. Done through her to him. That crumpled plane. That crumpled body.

'So beautiful here in the fall. Those lower hills, the crimson maple—'

But the crimson had dried by the time they found him.

'Change your thinking glasses,' the nurse inside ordered Donna. Swiftly she did, to find the outer world a vast bowl filling with burnt umber light, the maligned mountains jet black towers against the western sky.

'We'll be arriving about dinner time.' The patient sighed. 'But I believe you have everything on my diet list and any specialties you may require. My sisters are quite apt to make this a welcome-home-bad-child affair and, when they do—' Lifted hands expressed her concept of the menu.

Donna nodded, then took a left fork

supposed to come out on a two-lane county roadway. How revealing was a person's vocabulary! Take that welcome-home bit. The five sisters had all been married, all had had homes of their own, yet all had returned to the old Morgan mansion when death or divorce or, in two cases, marriage of their children had robbed them of companionship.

Why there? She wondered why each had not created an independent life of her own. Ah, well, it was none of her business.

Donna swished her car across a bridge, a river purling below, then noticed on the far side the fan-like flounce of harvested row-crops. So many torn lace ruffles, she would have described them.

'If you'll stop on this rise—'

Obediently Donna stopped the car and uttered a tiny gasp of amazement. Ahead, like a vast fan, terminating in an intersecting purple mountain, lay fields of grain. Green, golden, tan, an extension of the smaller fan on the river banks.

'The Morgan estate,' proclaimed Mrs Montel proudly. 'You turn in at those pillars. They are not the ones Great-grandfather established there. Someone,' she stressed the word, 'destroyed the originals. These are merely pseudo-malachite brought from lava beds in the eastern part of the state.'

Again Donna responded to the order.

Then when they had topped another small rise, she obeyed the brief, 'Wait here. See ahead?'

Donna Maria sought for descriptive words: unbelievable, grandiose (she couldn't say beautiful) and finally, 'How striking.' For it was. That mammoth mansion ahead seemed a machete with polished blades.

In a moment a vagrant cloud slid across the sun's path and the cruelty of the scene vanished, the vast mansion acquiring a muted tone of beauty.

She recalled what she had been told about Morgan Manor. The original Martin Morgan had come to this country from his native land. He had suffered bitter poverty. Eventually he had filed on western homesteads and married in succession, with death between, two women. Then, when hundreds of acres of now productive farm land lay around him, he learned he had inherited wealth in his native land.

This house, this mansion was a material symbol of his superiority, his defiant effort to 'show these Westerners' how the aristocracy of his land lived.

Not that he had lived to enjoy his triumph! A slight earth tremor, and a glazed triforium, insecurely set, had shot down, pinning him beneath it.

His son, now a motherless lad, had found him and accepted his final words—words he lived and died by. With no son, only five girls to inherit, he had yet laid down the dictum.

Donna Maria wondered what it was and if it were worth the price.

Again they moved forward and again stopped as Mrs Montel cried, 'There he is; there is my boy. Honk, Nurse, honk!'

As though on a swivel, a far away head turned. To Donna Maria, it seemed the man's body strode toward them on mammoth legs. Not until he reached a clearing did she realize he was riding a mower and had lifted the cutter-length bars for a more rapid approach.

With only a touch of curiosity, she saw him near, turn off the ever increasing volume of sound, then stride toward them. This, then, was the 'son'—Hank he was called—who managed the Morgan Ranch. Obviously, in this field of endeavor the manager participated in the labor.

He had grey eyes, sweat-tousled hair beneath a billed cap. As he approached, Hank's attention was fixed on Donna Maria.

'How is she really?' he demanded of her. And before she could reply, 'She's not in an ambulance as I ordered.'

'Hank,' soothed Mrs Montel, 'come see what Nurse fixed up for me here; my leg is all cozied.'

'You won't leave?' His voice had dropped. Then as he found Mrs Montel's attention fixed on her swollen leg, 'I must talk to you alone, soon,' he whispered.

There was another searching, penetrating look, and this Hank or Henry Emerson strode around the front of the car to Mrs Montel.

Donna Maria sat transfixed, feeling somehow as though she had been hypnotized, pierced by that searching glance as if by a hypodermic with lethal but pleasing contents. Then she shook her head and said stiffly, 'If you don't mind, Mrs Montel needs rest immediately.'

'See you at dinner,' was Emerson's retort. And Donna Maria didn't bother to tell him she doubted it, that Mrs Montel would be dining from a tray in her suite of rooms.

Driving away, she realized he had directed this at her and looked back. He was smiling triumphantly, she thought angrily, because he had finally gotten through to her and made her realize to whom she had been speaking.

Janice Montel leaned back—a soft sigh revealing a release from tension. 'Isn't he wonderful,' she stated rather than questioned. 'I don't know how we could have managed without him.' So efficient; above all, so painstakingly honest.

'The earlier ranch managers, y'know, were so busy feathering their own nests, only pin-feathers were left for my sisters to

10

subsist on.'

Later Donna would learn more. Now she merely looked at the mansion they were nearing, wondering which of several approaches to use.

'The main driveway—yes, there. See, they are bringing out the chair. My, the people that has carried in and out of the manor.'

Donna glanced up, now that her route had been cleared. Amazing that any edifice as great, as imposing as this could carry such an aura of gloom. Probably the early evening light. It was too early for those tall metal stanchions to blossom, too late for any sunset gleam to touch the ramp.

Faces. So many witches, Donna thought half hysterically. But now as she drew up they swooped down and became individualized.

Names. Would she ever fit the names to the faces. How could so many sisters be so unlike? Was she being introduced to each according to age or to importance?

Norah Morgan Norton, a large woman who discarded Donna with her glance.

Louella Morgan Borden, ingratiating—a subtle smile, a warning flash to the nurse.

Helena Morgan Cartwright, obviously hard of hearing, questioning, covering up what?

And · Fanetta Morgan Elbert, forthright—or was she? Wasn't this rather a

11

pose?

And why the mention of Morgan with each introduction?

Voices like the buzz of many insects. Dinner was ready to be served. They'd wheel her right in before everything became too cold, too sodden to enjoy. She'd been forever reaching there. Why hadn't she taken the ambulance 'the boy' had ordered?

Donna Maria glanced at her patient. The lovable, happy woman of half an hour ago had vanished. In her place was a rapidly shriveling facsimile, blanched of face, trembling.

'I am sorry.' Donna Maria spoke above the buzz. 'My patient needs rest. I shall serve what is listed on her diet in—'

'And just who do you think you are?' demanded Mrs Norah Norton.

'The nurse appointed by Mrs Montel's physician to assure the patient she need not be returned to the hospital for further treatment. Insofar as a nurse may be able to attend her patient—'

Ah, that had struck home, though as yet she could only guess at the reason.

'But you will dine with us,' stated Mrs Norton.

'Thank you.' Donna Maria smiled at her. 'It will be a pleasure.' For hadn't she spotted the lurking figure of Emerson behind a portiere?

CHAPTER TWO

Henry Emerson stepped forward, mouthed greetings, then addressed Donna Maria. 'I'll take over. I can handle that invalid chair better than any of the rest of you.'

In-valid? Donna's mind caught the odd pronunciation of the word, and gratefully she stepped back. She had viewed that Alpine flight of steps with misgivings, yet knew Mrs Montel's 'suite' was on an upper floor.

'I'll return for the luggage,' Emerson informed her, 'yours as well as hers. Suggest you girls go on with your dinner; I won't be long.'

'Hank, did you check the wheat price today?' Norah posed the question.

'Naturally.'

'You sold? I mean with bumper crops this year—'

'And this year's not yet over. Comfortable, Mother?'

He made the upward trek easily, almost, Donna thought, as though he were pulling the canvas and wheeled atrocity up a ramp.

She glanced back once. Below, the four 'Morgan girls' stood as though transfixed, immobile; then as one they wheeled and moved down the hall.

Later Donna might check the numerous

paintings that seemed to mount the staircase with her and, below, the tall, imposing furniture, so old, so unusual, so beautiful. Currently her mind was on her patient and the effect this homecoming could have upon her.

Emerson's immediate actions surprised Donna a little. He actually tested the bed, lying down, rolling across the broad expanse, then double-checking beneath the bed as though he might find some hidden monster.

'All right,' he reported as he slipped his arms beneath Mrs Montel's armpits, and with Donna Maria guiding the malfunctioning legs, slid her into bed.

'Ah,' breathed the patient.

Donna Maria nodded, puzzled. What could be restful about this particular room? It was packed with furniture, some pieces tiered above others. In the small hall that led to the suite, there had barely been room for the invalid chair to pass.

How dreary, had been her first reaction. Now she added, How confusing. For those walls, too, were a hodgepodge of pictures, portraits, landscapes, even enlarged photographs beautifully framed.

'You relax,' Emerson ordered Mrs Montel after Donna Maria had removed the light coat and small squash hat from the patient, and substituted warm slippers for the leather ones she had demanded for the trip. 'I'll

14

show the nurse around.'

He did. He enumerated rooms. 'Bathroom,' he said, and Donna shuddered. Imagine anyone, even with flexible legs, getting into that high-rise marble atrocity. And the greyness of the room, the dreariness—

'Sitting room.'

But where was there room left to sit? Here, too, furniture seemed to have had modern offspring that nipped at parental legs.

'I should explain. Mother brought all of her furniture from our home to the Manor after Father's death, as did the other girls. And while we were not wanting for storage space in stable, barn and many sheds, once their stoves, refrigerators and wash and dry equipment were tucked in, there was room for nothing else.

'Now if you'll step out here—'

Donna Maria stepped, then froze. She had passed through opened French doors to a narrow balcony, and ahead, overpowering everything within sight, were those mountains, grim, foreboding.

'Ah-ah,' Emerson's voice warned, and a bit ostentatiously he reached before her to a line of iron palings which, had she leaned against them, would have thrown her sixty feet to a stone terrace.

For a long moment he looked at her, seeming to search her very soul.

15

'I am asking you at the dinner table to tell me you found a loose stretch of paling on the balcony. You are to request I fix it as soon as possible. Agreed?'

Silently Donna Maria held out her hand, found it caught in a vise-like grip, then dropped it.

'Mother can roll herself out here and will. You will check daily?'

Then, just as her mind had built up a morbid possibility, he added, 'In old houses like this, erosion strikes.'

A moment later Mrs Montel cried, 'Hank, your legs again—'

'Just tendon tension, Mother.'

'Fight or flight?' quipped Donna, the words flying from her before she could control them.

He wheeled on her. 'Nurse has a possible cure?' he asked sardonically.

Donna smiled wryly. 'Sorry; that got away from me. I could tell you one patient's cure. He was a tough old boy. He decided he, not the other fellow, would be the one to determine the time for fight or flight.'

Again the long steady glance, then a sharp nod that was in a sense an expression of approval. 'You'll be how long getting Mother settled in? Fed? Then join us below stairs.'

'Half an hour.'

In another moment he was gone, Donna

16

watching the hard leanness, lines, rather like those of this Gothic monstrosity to which he'd been at least temporarily doomed.

She turned then to what was to her an amazing appurtenance: a tiny, very tiny kitchenette, the likes of which she would find in each suite of rooms. A basin with hot and cold water. A metal table of three tiers; the top carrying an electric plate, the other two everything from frying pan to percolator to waffle iron.

Above was a compact set of shelves, barren now but later to be filled with purchases Mrs Montel had ordered while in the city hospital.

Swiftly she assembled her patient's evening meal. It was simple, yet she managed to serve it in an appetizing manner. For she had learned through her studies that where emotional illness was concerned, sight and aroma were as important to digestion, if not more important, than the actual ingredients.

'Nurse,' cried Mrs Montel, 'this is like a picnic. Now, if you'll open those blinds so I can watch the sunset on the mountains. Such fun, you know—the clouds trying to get away, then finding themselves dipped in orange or scarlet, or, at times, yellow. One can almost taste them.'

A moment later she added, 'Smells so appetizing.' And no one told her that her

17

reactions to scents had been tabulated; those she associated with fear and anxiety becoming taboo until her strength returned, those she saluted as reminders of gay days pinpointed for moments which might carry stress.

And then she said anxiously, 'Dear, do run along before my sisters start steaming.'

Donna Maria, having changed into uniform, stood for inspection, and her patient nodded. 'That will keep them in their place,' she whispered. 'Dear, I'll be quite all right. I'll even—' she hesitated as though afraid to voice this—'be happy.'

A cautious look around the suite, and Donna started on toward her meeting with the family. Surely one needed a road map or house map in such an edifice as this.

Or a guide. Louella Morgan Borden met her at the foot of the stairs. Slyly she smiled. 'Imagine being a nurse. An alibi for everything. My sisters simply can't condemn you for being late.'

'Late?' Donna took up the challenge. 'Sorry; I hadn't heard dinner being announced.'

'Oh, we don't.' Louella had slid back in her superiority. 'I mean, naturally we can't conduct ourselves currently as we did when Father was alive. Servants,' she explained. 'We have none. They are so dreadfully expensive these days.'

18

Donna glanced at a gilt-carved bureau bookcase that stood at the end of the hall and smiled. Sold, that could underwrite a retinue.

'We dine in here,' Mrs Borden said, and turned to a rear doorway. 'It was a rear sitting room, but none of us are getting any younger and—well, it is much closer to the kitchen.'

'And charming,' added Donna honestly.

Bathed as it was now in the afterglow, everything within the room took on a rich luster. Even Henry Emerson, who waited to seat her. Did they observe such seating protocol, she wondered, when no stranger was present? She would learn in time.

Emerson, she assumed had made a concession: a light jacket. Donna, thinking of harrowing days in the beating sun, wondered. She would learn he ordinarily had his evening meal later, in a lean-to some distance away.

A swift look around the long table. Definitely à la carte, Donna thought, remembering each sister had her own preferences. And hers? She instinctively gestured toward Emerson's plain steak, browned potatoes and gravy, broccoli, sliced tomatoes. She wondered a little as this or that sister begged her to try a bowl thrust at her or said 'I know you'd enjoy this.'

And if she thought she was being slightly

ridiculous, checking to see if those offering ate of what they offered, a glance at Emerson and a slight nod from him proved her caution advisable for some reason. What?

Oh, perhaps he knew they went a bit far in their seasoning and wanted the digestive system of his mother's nurse undisturbed.

'Now—' all were bent on ingesting dinner when Norah Morgan Norton spoke—'you will give us an exact report of our sister's condition. From the beginning, please.'

Please? But this was an order and delivered as such from one who, Donna thought, was not accustomed to being disobeyed.

What could reach her most quickly? Donna scanned the woman's formidable features; the normally large eyes were narrowed. And then she noted certain discrepancies. Mrs Norton, wearing no more than a glamorized housedress, also had on pearls.

'Really—' Donna's brows arched— 'suppuration is hardly a subject for dinner table consumption, is it?'

A look of unholy glee swept across Emerson's face, one of frustration across that of Mrs Norton.

'I hadn't realized. Then after—'

'After my patient is asleep, I shall come down and relay Dr Haskell's report and his orders.'

Then she glanced at Emerson. 'I found a length of the grilled iron paling on the balcony loose. I imagine I should ask you to check and see it is repaired?'

'I'll call Foster's Metal Repair in the morn—'

'Hank,' Fanetta Morgan Elbert's voice was sharp, 'you know we can't afford an expense such as that might be.'

'Can we afford hospitalization and possible surgery for Mother should she, in a careless moment, crash through and sustain multiple fractures?'

Silence settled for a moment like a heavy cloud; then Fanetta's sharp voice slashed it. 'We are paying a nurse to see that our sister does nothing foolish, aren't we?'

As one they turned toward Donna, but she was aware only that Emerson was demanding something of her.

'Really,' she drawled, 'in an edifice such as this one doesn't anticipate lethal negligence, does one?'

'Hank,' Norah rapped the order, 'call Foster the first thing tomorrow morning. If you don't, I shall.'

Donna's attention was caught and held by the one heretofore silent sister, Helena Morgan Cartwright. Ah, hard of hearing. Why? Interesting.

'Oh, do close those blinds,' she said petulantly. 'Such a glare—'

21

Glare? With the sun so far to the west its presence was no more than a memory? Covertly Donna watched the woman, estimated her age as compared to the ages of the other sisters.

'Helena—' Norah, obviously the oldest of the family, spoke heavily—'is so sensitive to everything, sight, sound, aroma.' She shook her head half in admiration, half in exasperation.

But if she were hard of hearing, how could she be sensitive to sound?

Fanetta, seeing the doubt, spoke quickly. 'Highly pitched sound,' she elucidated, 'simply splits her head, whereas she can barely hear a normal pitch. Interesting, don't you think, Nurse?'

'Most interesting,' Donna returned. But only Henry and perhaps one other caught the implication and looked alert.

Light blossomed, and Donna blinked. Surely the muted sunset was less glaring than the sharp beam of the chandelier above the table. One glance, and she estimated again the cost of that group of lights nestled in intricately interwoven sheaths of brass. And this was a lesser room!

Crops and weather, crops and neighbors were discussed, then crops again, until Donna wondered how Henry Emerson could dine at all. No wonder he preferred dinner in a lean-to.

She watched the others dip into the small dishes encircling their dinner plates and hid a smile. Diversity of tastes when all had been reared here on the same viands? Well, time did strange things. To strange people?

A bit laboriously each stacked her own dishes on an individual tray, carried them to the kitchen, then returned with her preferred dessert. With Henry, Donna had accepted green apple pie and thought it excellent.

The meal had been both a trial and a revelation. No, indeed, she would not remain there a day longer than was necessary, and if in the meantime she could arrange to take her meals elsewhere, say with her patient, she would do so.

Or would she? Could she have learned as much about each had she met them one at a time and under any other circumstances? And why was it important she should?

'If you will excuse me,' Emerson's voice broke in. Then he added, 'Nurse?' Donna saw he was standing, and in a moment both were following shy little sly little Louella Morgan Borden from the room.

They caught up with her half hidden by a pedestal holding an ornate Greek figure.

'Oh,' she breathed, 'I was just running up to bid sister good night.'

'May I carry the message?' Donna returned. 'Even a pleasant interruption in her rest would not be good at this time.

And,' she smiled, 'a comfortable night to you.'

'Comfortable—' A sob, and Louella turned and ran back down the hallway.

Emerson motioned Donna on; then when they reached a landing, 'She and slumber are not en rapport,' he commented dryly. 'She roams the house and the garden, and the only reason she doesn't break her fool neck is that she carries not a flashlight, but a set of them.' A sober head shake concluded his summation.

Donna waited until she had checked on her patient, sleeping quietly, then joined Emerson on the small gallery to find him with a flash light of his own, checking the iron paling.

The world outside was now drenched in twilight, and the small beam picked up an area where the paneling had broken away. Erosion? There was almost no brown rust. There was sharp brown and gray markings where, Donna thought, someone's screwdriver had slipped under pressure.

Nothing was said by either. Emerson disappeared a moment, then returned with a coil of wire. Carefully he secured the paling in place; then he straightened.

'My room, when I use it,' he confided softly, 'is directly across the hall. But I suggest locking the main door to your suite. We also have a somnambulist.'

A lift of his head, a sudden wariness in his mien, and he motioned her inside, saying in a louder voice he would have the metal repair man check all the galleries and also have him determine the cause.

Inside, well away from the sleeping Mrs Montel, he looked at Donna earnestly. 'I must talk to you away from here and alone. I feel you realize there is something here I can neither uncover nor handle. Are you willing to meet me and discuss this and then remain silent until—'

Willing? All she wanted to do at that precise moment was turn and run. But how futile. She wouldn't be able to live with herself if she did not try to see this through.

And then? Well, what had evasion done for her thus far? That mountain peak, black against the southwest window, reared in warning.

'I can arrange an impromptu shopping trip.'

'Don't advertise in advance or you won't ride alone. Say ten-thirty at Newton's Drugstore. He's good at understanding. He'll let us retreat to his den behind the store proper.'

He was gone. Donna latched the door, pushed a bolt—newly installed, she noticed—then tiptoed through to the gallery and stared out in dismay, apprehension and wonder.

There were hundreds of acres of land: valleys, trees lining roadways like tiny French knots. And they had to meet in town? A small town no more than fifteen to twenty miles away, yet—

She shivered a little, then squared her shoulders. By tomorrow night at this time she would have more knowledge of the situation, be able to determine whether she was or was not the right person to care for the patient.

CHAPTER THREE

Donna Maria Caffery slept little that first night. But that was not unusual. Each edifice, were it cottage or palace, had its own sounds, strange sounds. And being different from the ones the subconscious had learned to accept as normal, they brought one up from slumber.

'I look better than you this morning,' Mrs Montel greeted her.

Donna explained her concept of new sleeping areas, and the patient accepted it. 'With me,' she confided, 'it was finally being at home. I love this silly old place—I think.'

Donna let that ride and was rewarded with an elucidation.

'If only I could unpack and spread my own

things around,' she fretted. 'But there simply is no room. Great-grandfather had a thing about possessions. I could almost swear he even nailed the paintings to the walls. He wanted nothing, but nothing, changed.'

That had been all right when she and the others were young, but after they had married, and had homes of their own they naturally wanted symbols of that era around them.

Mrs Montel had the symbols, but they were all securely packed, crated and stacked, impeding any free movement one might attempt while traversing the suite. True, she had tossed woven afghans over some, had fitted cretonne over pads and put ruffles over others, yet there was a sense of being literally packed into rooms with inanimate objects.

'What did you say?' demanded the patient.

'Oh, just my generation speaking,' Donna replied. On being pressed, she admitted she had asked, 'Is it worth it?'

'Well—' new spirit sounded in the patient's voice—'that is what all of my sisters have done. Each of them has her personal belongings in her particular suite. Why, to tell you the truth, you have to walk sideways to get into Helena's sitting room.'

'How fortunate each of you has a suite,' murmured Donna, and pressed her lips tightly over a follow-up of 'Or is it?'

Mrs Montel seemed to catch the

implication and defensively said that in the beginning, the first sisters to return 'home' had stored in the carriage house. Then she added the cliché which had always made Donna wonder.

'But things turned up missing.'

The nurse in Donna drew not a red herring but a shopping pad across the delicate subject. She asked if it would not be advisable to jot down items one might want or need as one thought of them. Then, if somebody were running into town, they might be picked up.

'Clams,' stated Mrs Montel. 'There is nothing I crave more than clam fritters. But my sisters can't bear the odor of sea fish. Take crab Mornay. What is more delectable? But here—'

'Here,' stated Donna firmly, 'we can prepare what we please, providing, of course, we can find the fresh shell fish. And no one who is not invited during that period need know or, knowing, have the temerity to question your choice.'

'I do believe I could eat with relish,' murmured Mrs Montel. 'You know my husband was a fisherman in a sense. We lived at the coast. My, such a time as I had learning to prepare his favorite dishes, a challenge I thoroughly enjoyed.'

It was her chance; Donna leaned close. 'Promise not to tell. I'll slip out and pick up

28

whatever has been brought from the coast, and tonight we'll live it or eat it up.'

'Oh, my dear. And it will be within my diet?'

'Definitely. Your Vitamin C intake will even be increased, and there is nothing in the food you want that will not be an asset.'

Donna's spirits dropped when, upon hearing a noise at the door, she found Henry Emerson affixing a Yale lock. Norah and other sisters were watching him suspiciously.

'For your protection,' he informed them. 'I want to place them upon each. You all read or heard of that recent case where a woman, living with her own family—'

Swiftly they assented. The house was large and lonely, and in this crazy age anyone could slip in, hide, then wreak havoc after sleep destroyed their waking awareness of strangers.

Yet Donna wondered. A Yale lock at a time like this meant her patient need not be disturbed during her swift trip to town and the conference with Henry Emerson. It also meant Mrs Montel would be there alone during that period.

Anxiously she looked from one sister to the other and found no answer, and had to remind herself she could be taking this too seriously.

At the blare of a horn below, Emerson straightened. 'I'll see to the other rooms later. Have to take that load into the warehouse now.' And he was off.

'I do wish Father had seen fit to establish a silo and warehouse here,' muttered Louella.

'You know very well why he didn't,' snapped Fanetta. 'He'd have had to allow a railroad to run in a spur track, and you know how he felt about rights of way. Sacrosanct.'

Donna whisked away, reported the conference and actions in the hall, then picked up the list. 'I'll take the door key with me. You settle down. And, Mrs Montel, do not go onto the balcony; your chair might get away from you. Hank will have those palings fixed before night. Promise?'

Solemn but inwardly disturbed, the woman held out her too chubby hand.

Donna sped out, down the steep stairway and through a door she hoped would lead her to the general area of a carport built off the carriage house.

She had reached her car when she was stopped.

'And just where do you think you are going while on duty?' demanded Fanetta Elbert.

Donna waved the list. 'To pick up some necessary articles my patient overlooked in the city. Now if you'll move from the back of the car—it shoots to the rear with astonishing rapidity.'

She saw that it did, though her breath was

held until she found it hadn't even grazed the suddenly alert Fanetta. Perhaps she had learned a lesson: that this nurse meant what she said.

How beastly hot it was, Donna thought, heading her car east by north. The one advantage she could allow that magnificent architectural atrocity behind her: it did insulate.

On either side great stands of wheat bowed their heads in prayer that they might be harvested soon. But that, Emerson had intimated, had been the kind of a year it was. You planted a seed, turned around, and there it was full grown, pleading to be taken at its moment of fulfillment.

A U turn of the road, and Morgan Manor appeared for a moment, a bit like baled hay, but with spikes shooting upward and, she wondered, filled with some gaseous element which might explode?

Don't be ridiculous, she chided herself; it's really more like a fortress. And the inner voice jeered, 'But with the foes within and inwardly mobilized.'

Ah, she topped a hill and looked down. Ahead lay the small town, main streets like spokes all seeming to center on the grain warehouse that would dwarf even Morgan Manor if placed beside it.

Estimating the time, she shopped first at a supermarket, then went to the Newton

Pharmacy and, as she was in uniform, sans cap, seemed to be recognized instantly.

'Back here.' Newton, the pharmacist, indicated a passage to the rear of the drug area. 'Fine; just give me your list.'

A small den for occasional private life, Donna thought. Henry Emerson was pacing its length.

'Did you fly?' she asked.

'Had another take the truck on to the warehouse. Nurse, exactly how do you feel about the Morgan menage?'

'How I feel and what I know are in two different categories. As you must realize, Mr Emerson, in my profession we run tests before we accept any diagnosis. If you will give me some background—'

He threw up both hands.

'Then tell me how you got into this,' she suggested. For in what better way could she read the interrelationships of the Morgans?

'Oh, well.' He started by answering questions she placed adroitly, even as she watched his expression when he replied. 'Monny Montel owned a charter boat,' he began. 'I was around twelve when he took Mother and Dad and me and others out on a deep sea fishing trip.

'Came one of those storms, and the ship foundered and went down. Mother and Dad went with it. Monny seemed obsessed with saving me. He did. Then when he found

32

there was literally no insurance or family to take me, he took me home to his wife, your patient.

'They adopted me, reared me, gave me everything within their power, from love to education.'

Swiftly Donna's mind had kept pace. Many sea-loving city businessmen achieved their dream of a deep sea fishing smack by using this as a charter boat; they were paying guests who underwrote the initial cost of the vessel.

'I was doing my stretch in Viet Nam when Dad Montel—I called him that—died. He went over the side of the *Sea Queen* with a heart attack, in the way he would have preferred.

'When I came home I found Mother Jan bereft financially and in every other way. She wanted to "go home." Home to her was the old Morgan place.

'I'd visited there as a kid. Old Mr Morgan was still alive, and somehow he indoctrinated me with a yen to study agriculture. In college I went all out.

'But when I took Mother Jan out there, I found the Morgan girls living on the past and little else. The ranch managers they had had, careless or worse, had manipulated crops in such a way that they rather than the sisters benefited.'

He paused, and Donna placed a question.

33

'Well, why didn't they sell? You say their father had died during your time overseas.'

'They couldn't,' he stated flatly, 'and they can't. Until every Morgan sister but one is dead, there can be no disposition made of the estate.'

'And there are five living,' breathed Donna, and tucked the thought away.

He had learned what the current estate manager was doing, had revealed it, had had the man chucked out, and the sisters and his Mother Jan had begged him to take over.

'Well,' he shrugged, 'after Viet Nam, after seeing hunger and hopelessness at its lowest ebb, what else could I do?'

The first year had been a 'boom,' the second excellent. Even dividing the money five ways, each had had enough for the first time in years.

'And you, as an agriculturist, were enjoying every moment on every acre,' murmured Donna.

Stiffly he reared. 'I loathe every acre of that entire seven hundred odd,' he intoned. 'I live for the day I can ride off free of it, completely free physically and psychologically.'

'Where?' she mused rather than asked.

'Give me the sea, where one doesn't have to depend upon machinery to get one there; just the rhythmic pacifying beat of waves on the shore without banshees screaming you're

34

wasting your time.'

She could have suggested that sans muscles one could not row far and would be beached without a gasoline engine or motor of some kind to pick up when a man's muscles gave out. She didn't. She was seeing below to the devastating weariness of the man who ran the Manor.

Automatically, as a result of her training, she evaluated the words of the man talking to her. He had suffered, as a young boy, a devastating emotional bereavement. The Montels had stepped in. He had known they were not responsible for the freak storm which had destroyed his parents and their boat. He had been saved, cared for, above all, loved.

How else repay this great debt he owed but by doing what he had been trained to do, taking over the Morgan grain ranch which, for some reason, he instinctively hated?

'Why you—' he hesitated—'you understand.'

Donna smiled. 'Go on. I do, I think. Yet something new has been added. You said no disposition could be made of the Morgans' inheritance—'

'Until only one, the last one, is left alive,' he intoned.

'You'd like your Mother Jan—'

His expletive literally shook the vials from nearby shelves. No! Nothing was worth the

35

life led in that house, that 'House of Hate' slipped from him.

'But she feels she owes it to her sisters, to her now dead parents, one might say to herself, to see it through until "her time has come."'

And, Donna might have added, she uses you, the innocent victim. Why had he been made to feel his indebtedness to the Montels as he had? Interesting; worth running down.

He stood up then. 'You'd better be getting back.'

'Mr Emerson, you had some reason for suggesting this meeting. Please be frank for your sake, your Mother Jan's and,' she added carefully, 'for my own. You fear something. What is it?'

His answer came quickly. 'I do not know,' he confessed. 'But after I had met you, caught that certain something in your eyes, I knew I had to, that I could talk to you freely. I've never felt anything like that with anyone before,' he added.

Carefully Donna evaluated aloud. 'There is nothing in the phlebitis your mother was hospitalized for that could have triggered your apprehension.

'Concede the loosening of the iron palings could have been an alert. You say all sisters may live out their lives at the manor. That is and has been their symbol of home. What then do you fear?'

'Home!' He spat the word. 'There is not one of them who doesn't hate that house as much as I; not one who might not sacrifice honor, conscience, call it what you will, to be rid of that monstrosity and be free.'

CHAPTER FOUR

The blare of a horn, and Emerson gave a salute, then rushed out the rear door of the pharmacy. Donna turned the other way. What kind of a mind did she have, she wondered, that it had picked up yet another possibility?

Should her patient be the one to outlive the others, wouldn't Emerson inadvertently benefit?

Newton, watching, seemed to be running her suspicions through some mystical test tube. That nurse needed clarification of some type. Nothing he could offer from his neat laboratory, but what about that inner lab he carried above his black brows?

'Too bad,' he commented heavily, waving others aside that he might wait on her, 'just too bad there aren't more men like young Emerson around. Talk of people being unselfish, that lad is selfless.'

'Selfless?'

'Noticed how lean he looked, didn't you?

Well, year or so ago they had a virus out there. Manifested itself as infectious hepatitis. Couldn't bring in enough aides to see the old girls through, and he took over. Night duty.

'He also ran down the cause, and when they would not okay a new water supply, he dug down in his army back-pay savings and had a new well dug. Has it serviced now by state so it can't occur again.'

'Thank you,' breathed Donna.

The gray-blue eyes twinkled. 'Might fatten him up a little to know he has a friend in that menage.'

She would be there only a short time, only until Mrs Montel could function without tri-daily dressings, use her mottled legs.

Or would she be there only that long? And who wouldn't have an antipathy to food if he had to eat in the atmosphere in which she had dined the previous night?

'Will see what can be done,' she murmured.

'Had a feeling you would, or he wouldn't have risked meeting you here. Now these—' he pushed forward the anti-coagulant capsules—'should ease the patient.'

True pharmacists were not supposed to comment on prescriptions. He was risking his standing. Impulsively she held out her hand, seemingly signing some pact between them.

Donna drove off into the heat of the late morning. Steam heat, she might have called it, yet when she began passing grain ranches she saw the chaff from the combines rising, and when she was near enough she coughed a response.

The mountains, she thought, were down, perhaps also burdened by man-made pollution, though that was vital to the survival of the grain and therefore of the human of the species.

Ah, well, squashed as they seemed, they posed less of a threat to her peace of mind.

Off the country highway and onto a secondary road, and she came to a grinding stop. Just ahead stood a high, long black car, looking more like a mortician's mourners' carriage than anything else.

Yet just in front, where the hood seemed to list, was a familiar figure: Norah Morgan Norton on her poor arthritic knees in the road.

Donna sprang to the rescue and slowly, carefully eased the older woman up to where she could rest against the car.

'A flat,' she reported unnecessarily. 'When no one passed, I thought I'd change it. I used to change tires. But now—' She held out hands grotesque in their stiffened curvature.

'I'll run you home, feed my patient; then if we can find no one to take care of this, I'll return. Or was your business in town important?'

'Not now,' came the revealing response, hurriedly covered with, 'what is important these days? I strive and strive.' Even her tonal quality was arthritic, stiff, defiant.

A moment's silence; then, 'Nurse, you do understand, don't you? I am the only one of the Morgan girls who really cares. I am dedicated to seeing this—this—'

'This what?' Donna's tone asked for more than a surface answer.

'Well, this maintaining a home for our families. Suppose there was a war or a depression. All of the Morgans and their children could be harbored there. Someone simply must keep the others in line. As I am the eldest, that duty falls on me.'

They were now out in a land of gold and russet, with a few patches of green. The mountains were little more than a dust-dyed ruffle on the horizon.

'Hmm,' mused Donna lightly, 'what would you do if you hadn't this burden to carry? I mean, just for fun?'

'Fun?' she echoed as though she'd never before heard the word. And after a moment, 'Oh, yes, fun. Well, I did have a flair for ceramics. Had instruction, even bought my own kiln. But now—' Her crooked hands were evidence that avenue was closed.

She sketched her later years briefly. After her husband's sudden death, her ailing father

40

had sent for her. So she and her children had moved to the manor house, the first Morgan girl to return. Then her father had died, her two children married and moved away, 'clear out of the state,' she cried in protest.

'They didn't enjoy living at the Manor?'

'Oh, by then Helena's husband had run off with some girl, and she brought her children home. They were so undisciplined mine could not tolerate them.'

So there need be no international war; the Morgan girls seemed able to produce their own.

'Nurse, there at your hospital, have you heard of any new, real cure for arthritis?'

Donna was now back in her car, and they speeded toward that sharply marked indenture which held the Manor. Truthfully she reported, 'I believe our physicians must first ascertain whether the disease is physical or psychosomatic.'

'How could it be that?' protested Mrs Norton, her voice rising.

'Have you ever been hospitalized, bedridden, for any period of time? You have? Do you remember how your legs felt when you again sought to use them? Stiff, unwieldy? Suppose you had, or your physician or nurse had allowed you to give in to the pain and distress.

'I am using this only as a broad example,' Donna hastened to say, 'but it does give

41

you—'

'Yes,' came in wonderment. Then, 'I can try—Oh, here we are. You are coming to lunch with me. No, I insist. You prepare my sister's tray, then—'

The great house now lay ahead, shrouded only at its base by vast hedges of boxwood, of cypress, of every known type of greenery which might be forced to conform to its lines.

Suddenly the woman beside Donna sat up. 'Look at her.' Her voice rose stridently, 'See what she's doing because I'm away. There are times when I could—'

Donna looked first at the two hands outstretched, curved to fit the neck of the woman slashing down a boxwood monstrosity which had blocked something from her, what, Donna did not yet know.

'Your hands,' murmured Donna, and like chunks of lead they dropped to the woman's lap. They shook even as did her shoulders, her entire body, in reaction from the killing rage which had obsessed her the moment before.

'You think—' Sobered, Mrs Norton spoke.

'I think I'd be darned if I'd let anyone or anything pour poison into my body. I wouldn't give either the power to sicken me for nothing. And it is really nothing in the last analysis. Laugh at it. Laugh at her if you can. Make your indifference an inner habit, lest you be triggered into an action you could regret, or sickness—'

She had pulled into the carport. For a scant moment she hesitated, wondering if she should say more, then noticed a panel truck not too far behind. The men from the metal works to repair the paling.

'Nurse—' heavy breathing preceded the word from Mrs Montel—'I am so glad you are here.' As Donna Maria rushed away, she refuted the thought personally. She wasn't glad to be in this House of Hate. Take that swift reaction of Mrs Norton. Given enough impetus, there could come a time when those arthritic hands could substitute something more malleable than the stiffened tendons.

Mrs Norton needed psychiatric treatment, but how many with her type of need recognized this or were willing to de-rationalize, having built up their own sense of righteousness under a given circumstance?

Suddenly fearful of what might have happened to her patient despite their precautions, Donna swooped up bundles and shopping bags. 'I can come down and talk to the men.'

'I shall send them up.'

'Give me five to ten minutes to ready Mrs Montel,' Donna begged, and set off at a brisk trot. It slowed before she reached the first landing.

Once in the hall, she really sped forward. Fanetta Elbert was crouched before the door of the Montel suite.

'I heard her calling,' she stated belligerently. 'You simply must leave an extra key with us when you go away from the Manor.'

Somehow she managed to insert her thin body into the packed small corridor before Donna could reassemble her packages. At that, when she entered, Fanetta stating she had been hearing calls of distress, she found Mrs Montel reclining, obviously enjoying a book she had asked be left there.

'Oh, Etta,' she protested, 'you're always hearing things, and they are always bad. You probably heard a crow singing in the east pasture.'

Fanetta strode past and opened doors to the balcony. In another moment she was back. 'You can't tell me that paling was loosened by erosion,' she charged.

'Dear, no one can ever tell you anything.'

'Mrs Elbert—' Donna was at her crispest in tone and attitude—'I must attend to my patient before the repair men come up.'

'You were gone long enough to attend to her a dozen times. If you ask me—'

A hand on the thin elbow, Donna steered her to the doorway, through it, then closed

44

the door and clicked the latch.

'Sorry,' she apologized to Mrs Montel, 'but I was a bit delayed. Your sister Norah Norton's car had a flat tire on the wrong stretch of the road.'

'That car,' sighed Mrs Montel. 'Surely we can afford another. Such strange things happen to this one. Take that day she was speeding down to contact her son, in port for only a few hours. And the car stopped smack in the center of the busiest highway.

'They found, of all things, dirt in the gasoline tank. How so much ever got in—'

Donna froze. She had specialed in a neighborhood where hoodlums had considered pouring dirt in gas tanks a lark. Her patient had been one of the victims when her comparatively new car came to a grinding halt at the wrong place in a busy intersection.

'I hope she bought a lock cap for the tank.'

'Well, Hank purchased one. I think he convinced her to keep her keys in a secret place.'

There; Donna was ready for the repair men and went to the door to find them just arriving, a bit somber, a bit curious. They had heard tell of 'this here place.' Quiet spot, but cool. Must be well insulated.

Soberly they accepted introductions to the patient, who watched them with interest and told them that balcony was a lifesaver for

45

her. Out there she could get away from chatter, petty quarrels, even the too loud radio of her sister who was hard of hearing.

One man signaled Donna outside and pointed out rusty scratches on the metal. 'Looks like someone was out to help her get away permanently,' he confided in a low voice. 'This was man or woman-done.'

'Woman,' stated his helper. 'Man would have checked, cleared those away. But why?'

Donna couldn't have given the answer in her mind. The repair man offered a solution. 'Could be her own balcony was getting slipshod. With this one in the hospital, could have figured to take these screws from here, maybe replace them later. Can't buy these across the counter these days, you know.'

It was a sane, sensible solution. Why, wondered Donna, couldn't she accept it? A woman like Fanetta wouldn't think further than to assure herself of her own safety.

Or had someone, say Hank, left this as a rust-red herring to throw her off the true scent?

Mr Newton's face flashed into her mind, and she shook her head. Men were inclined really to know men, and if that pharmacist believed in Hank as he did, she, a nurse, could accept his findings.

Oh, the utter relief of this.

Happily she turned to prepare lunch for her patient.

Low calorie cottage cheese well powdered with green onion package seasoning would bring a, 'Oh, this is delicious, Nurse.'

Donna thought about her adopted son Henry, or Hank. Newton had spoken for his lean look. It might be fetching on a television screen, but she, the nurse, had learned too little padding left nerve centers exposed in a sense, made them more acutely aware of distress.

It would be fun to cook for him. What could she possibly prepare up here and slip out to him? Sneak out, she corrected herself. And what made her think he'd accept?

Boiled cookies, she decided. If he'll sample them, he might be enticed to take some with him. Now where can I find peanut butter, oatmeal? And don't forget the glazed paper on which they harden, she reminded herself.

She was being ridiculous. Henry Emerson was not her patient. He was a mere acquaintance and would never, could never be more. Neither he nor any other man.

Depression as deep as her joy of a moment before swept in. But she would remain on a little longer than she had planned. She had to be of some use to her fellow-woman, to someone, to anyone, if she were to ease her own memories.

One by one the sisters came in as the repair men left for town and their lunch. One by one they looked curiously at the balcony, at their sister and at her nurse; above all at what 'that fool nurse,' as one called her, was serving 'Jan.'

Norah Norton was the last to enter. Politely she asked if her sister could spare the nurse for a half-hour or so. She had prepared lunch for the two of them. She would serve it in her suite. The other three were having 'one of their peculiar spells, all eating in their own rooms.' But it 'did save on dishwashing.'

'You have a very fine companion here,' she informed Mrs Montel as she was leaving. Then to Donna she said, 'In fifteen minutes if agreeable,' and left.

'Hmmm,' buzzed Mrs Montel. 'For one who usually fights like a bay steer when a nurse is brought home, her attitude has certainly changed. What did you do to her?'

Donna had to answer something, 'Possibly gave her an idea of a new therapy that relieves arthritic pains,' she evaded. 'My, what is that?' She stopped short. That noise could be nothing but a radio turned to its highest volume.

'That,' Mrs Montel grimaced, 'is my sister Helena working up an appetite for herself and ruining it for everyone else. I think if you close the balcony doors, Nurse, the sound may be muted a little.'

Helena the hard of hearing, thought

Donna, and almost wished she herself were.

'Earphones would make it easier on the rest of you,' she offered.

'I know. She knows. She refuses to use them. But such is the life of a multitude living under one roof.'

Meaning each had developed idiosyncrasies while away and, on returning, clung to them as symbols which set her apart from the others?

Donna was beginning to frame a picture of the relative position of the various suites. Norah Norton's entrance was exactly opposite the top landing. Next along the balcony was Louella Borden's, then the hard of hearing Helena Cartwright's, edging that of Fanetta Elbert. Donna blessed the linen and utility space which set Mrs Montel's a bit down the hall.

The tray removed, her patient comfortable, Donna started down that hall and came to a sharp stop.

Striding along the hall, her body one frozen ramrod, eyes glazed, came Fanetta Elbert. In her right hand, held out and up ready to strike was a heavy curved end fireplace iron.

'Wait,' called Donna.

'No,' came from between thinly set lips, 'I can't. I have had all I can stand. I am going to stop this if it's the last thing—'

The door opened. Helena stood there,

stood right in the path of the falling arc of iron.

CHAPTER FIVE

Even as Donna ducked low and sprang up to grasp the iron poker, she saw Mrs Cartwright's face, the grimace of triumphant pleasure. And for an insane moment she wondered why she had risked her own head to save this woman. Helena had known what she was doing to others, regardless of her hearing or lack thereof, and was glorying in her ability to wreck the peace of the afternoon.

'You can always move away, Fanetta,' she now said sweetly. 'Oh, is that my poker I've been missing? Nurse, I will take that.'

Swiftly Donna switched the rod to the other hand, then reached up and removed ear plugs from Helena's ears.

'Isn't that your poker in there at the fireplace?' she asked.

Fanetta, now aghast, stared, wheeled and started to run, but Donna was after her and reached the door to her suite as soon as she.

'I didn't mean to strike her,' Fanetta was sobbing; 'just to hit that radio until there wasn't a sliver of it left. Believe me, Nurse, truly, truly—'

'I believe you,' Donna soothed her. 'But had she tried to stop you—'

'I don't know, I don't know! I have to get out of here, Nurse, but where can I go?'

'Nurse,' Mrs Norton called from her doorway, 'are you ready? Really, just what is going on? Fanetta, you're not having another of your spells, are you?'

'I'll be with you in a moment.' Donna thrust Fanetta into her suite, then smiled at her. 'Go on, dear; have one of your spells. Like fainting, only you don't lose consciousness?'

'You know what they are?' came in shock.

'Yes. Remember the Biblical adage: "Resist not." I suggest you lie down, after locking your door. See that you are warm, evenly warm all over; then we'll find a way.'

'You mean—oh, you can't mean there is one?'

'I can, for there is. You're suffering from nerve exhaustion, a depletion of nerve energy. So salvage what you can while I lunch with your sister Norah. And don't think about what just did not happen.'

'How can I help—'

'Focus on something you'd adore to have happen.' She chanced to see a half finished water color on an easel. 'Envision that on display with customers, or patrons, fighting over which shall purchase it. Make it vivid, real!'

51

She heard the latch click on the door behind her, then turned even as a shaft of sunlight illuminated the long hall and touched stained-glass plates in a dome, bringing them to vivid color, swept across a tapestry, bringing it to life, and finally came to rest on the statue of a small boy, head up, triumph in every exquisitely wrought line.

Such beauty and such bitterness. So much wealth and such poverty of spirit. What a heritage had been left the Morgan girls. But why? If she only knew. Ah, but it was really none of her business, was it? She was there to attend Mrs Montel.

Yet did not healing the physical entail healing the conditions that had brought on the illness?

'Well, I do hope everything hasn't dried up,' was Mrs Norton's greeting.

A moment later she had pushed forward a maple chair, deeply cushioned, into which Donna sank gratefully, aware a tray lunch was in the offing.

'Taken all at once,' Mrs Norton spoke over her shoulder, 'we're rather a strong dose, aren't we? Can you tell me what occurred?'

'May I just say the ear-scratching noise of a radio seemed too much for the nerves of the person in the next suite?'

'Helena has always been like that.' Norah Norton spoke easily. 'She will do anything to call attention to herself. Even though she was whipped when she was tiny, she felt that a triumph, because she was being recognized as a member of the family.'

'Forever why?' breathed Donna.

'Well, Father could accept me as a girl; I am the oldest, you know. But when Helena followed and she too was a girl, perhaps he let his disappointment show. Not that he really neglected her, just overlooked her.'

'But those who followed—' protested Donna.

'I don't know. I can only assume he had become resigned to the inevitable.'

Mrs Norton brought out a casserole, spooning generous portions onto both plates: chicken and mushrooms with spicy notes of red and green pimiento against creamy-toned noodles. True, all out of cans, yet what ingenuity from this placid-appearing woman. And the salad was a poem of color in aspic.

'So comforting to have an appreciative audience.' The woman sighed happily as the hungry Donna lunched.

It was normal, even in this quiet atmosphere, for Donna's mind to slide back to that moment in the car when the hands, now working so deftly, had curved in a neck-throttling gesture; and from there to switch to the other sister, iron poker in hand, bringing it down, not on the offending radio but on the one who had turned it to its ear-splitting cadence.

Were they all—she choked on that thought. No, she with her knowledge could disseminate, throw the false to the winds, hold to the true. Not one of these, she reasoned, would willfully murder another. Yet thus far, in her short span here, she had seen an iron paneling which could send one crashing to a stone terrace; another with hands groped to choke life; a third with weapon raised.

Wasn't this indicative of all passion murders? Stress, built up over a long period of time, vented its overcharge, triggered by some overt act of another.

And in this House of Hate there had been years during which such passion had been building up.

Henry Emerson? Ah, didn't each know their very existence depended upon him?

Donna watched Mrs Norton with something akin to shock. The woman was actually enjoying herself.

Her mind flashed back to the scene in the car, the gesture which showed an inner desire to choke a sister. Donna had now identified her as Louella Borden, the one she as a nurse dubbed sly, ingratiating. She would always work quietly, pre-planning time and areas unobserved.

Interesting to learn why she had wanted

that shrubbery slashed off.

Donna learned within a few moments. To Mrs Norton's 'If you don't mind,' and 'Your legs are younger than mine,' the nurse hurried downstairs the better to hurry back up to her patient, then, nearly down the flight, was arrested.

From a small salon nearby came an anguished rendering of Schubert's *Unfinished Symphony*, played surely in the mood in which the poverty-stricken young musician had composed it, a lyric protest against life.

A glance inside showed Louella's head bowed over an ancient grand piano, light filtering in, half blocked by overgrown shrubbery.

Her errand completed, the nurse remembered she was one and had a case and hurried on to her patient to find her much more composed than Donna who was purportedly caring for her.

'Imagine Fanetta having the flutters,' she said conversationally. 'When they were small Helena used to sing in high falsetto to keep Fanetta awake. She'd scream, and she'd be the one scolded. I don't know why our maids or father never pinpointed the cause, the real cause.'

'Must have been a relief to her to get away.'

'My yes. If you ask me, I'd say that was why she ran off with a farm hand and brought father's wrath down on her—until he learned her husband was working to earn money for another college degree.'

'Then I assume her life with him was peaceful enough.'

It proved hardly that, according to her sister, and by the time she was through briefing the nurse on Fanetta's life, Donna wondered how she had lasted as long as she had without treatment.

A buzzer interrupted the finale, the sudden tragic death of Ed Elbert, and Mrs Montel took the telephone extension beside her bed.

'Yes, Henry. Yes, I am sure she won't mind.'

Hanging up, she said, unnecessarily, that had been Henry. Ordinarily he picked up the mail and brought it to the house, but this evening he was taking in another load of grain and wondered if Nurse Caffery would mind meeting him at the roadside and bringing it up.

'He meant in your car, of course. It will save him steps. You see, Nurse, he is the only one, save you, we trust with distribution of our mail.'

'You can't mean—'

Mrs Montel shrugged. 'We can't prove anything. But when whoever was near at postal delivery time picked up the mail, strange things happened. Letters, checks, even bills vanished into thin air, and naturally our rural delivery man couldn't pinpoint which day what arrived, could he?'

Poor Henry, thought Donna, and wondered if she should start thinking of herself in the same terms.

Well, there were a couple of hours or more before she was to drive down. At least she would be seeing him again, have a chance to analyze exactly why he affected her as he did. She'd hardly been able to blot him from her mind even during the hectic day she'd put in thus far.

The workmen came in, completed the securing of the railing, spoke of the weather. It was almost too hot to sit out there now, but later, when the sea breeze came up—

Mrs Montel decided on an afternoon television program which invariably, she confessed, put her to sleep. Why didn't Nurse Caffery visit Helena, see if she could find some way to make her want to keep that 'fool radio' tuned down?

But how could Donna get through to her? And who could tell if any reference to that subject might not trigger even further and shriller discordances?

'After I've checked on your sister, Fanetta,' Donna evaded. She stepped out of the suite and stepped back in. 'If you can communicate with her by telephone, perhaps you'd better prepare her. I doubt she would hear me knock.'

It took a moment before Fanetta replied, and Mrs Montel said she assumed she was wearing ear plugs. Which reminded Donna that Helena Cartwright, the one creating the din, had been wearing them when Fanetta had descended upon her.

Fanetta was at the door, both hands to her brow as though holding in its contents. 'I am going out of my head,' she cried.

'Why not go out of the house instead?' suggested Donna. 'I'd like a glimpse of the gardens. I know it's very hot, but there must be a cool spot.'

'And let her think she had driven me out?' came the protest.

'No, let her think we're having, if not afternoon tea, afternoon soda pop in a cool spot. Come on; I bought some this morning.'

The Morgan Manor grounds would have been beautiful in a city park. Here they showed signs of neglect which Fanetta promptly tried to cover up.

'Until Norah's hands and Janice's legs gave out, they did much of the work. Henry takes care of the basic upkeep, but not during harvest; there isn't time.'

'And you and the other two?'

'Norah feels we don't know enough about it. We were city dwellers. Oh, we tried, but it wasn't worth the effort, the other two criticized us so sharply.

'In fact,' she admitted, 'I began associating garden work with gastrointestinal distress.'

A corpulent Cupid aimed his arrow through an overgrowth of boxwood, and Donna felt her own fingers itch a little. How she would like to snip branches and release his charm to—to whom? Did anyone ever visit the garden?

'Oh, this is lovely,' she said, finding they had come to the edge of the formal area where the land slanted down into some timber and wild brush she couldn't recognize.

'The maligned gully.' Fanetta sighed. 'The boys must get that cleared out. People sneak in from the other side and picnic there. They're so thoughtless. They build small campfires and go off without covering them with dirt.

'Louella and I did our best to have the entire area cleared, but the other three voted us down. Nurse, about my nerves—'

'Why claim them as yours?' Donna asked lightly. 'Why not give them—' she caught herself in time—'oh, give them to that Cupid back there? When they start to vibrate, pretend you're running down there draping them around his stout little neck.'

'That's silly, but you know, it would be fun.'

'I don't know this is true in this case, but sometimes there are people who are in such desperate need of recognition of some kind—'

'I know: like those on TV newscasts who'll join anything if they feel they can get their pictures taken. Nurse, I am beginning to understand a little. But the awful noise—'

'Concede we're learning there is sound pollution. There can also be a means of building a sound-proof reception area. With proper foods—'

'Food!' she made a grimace.

'You mean you'd rather coil against noise, or brace in fear it may occur? If not, let me send for a book I have on nutritional experiments. Meanwhile, I am sure Mr Newton will give us adequate Vitamin B, especially twelves. Then with your nerves quieting down and your appetite picking up—'

They turned back to the Manor. Fanetta was thoughtful. Once she asked if it was true that this nerve sickness was not from a 'disordered brain.' And Donna wondered who had planted that thought.

'You mean it's psychosomatic rather than physical, and not a disorder in the sense the popular conception of that term might indicate. Rather, it's established habit reaction. Tell me a little of your life.'

She talked as they walked, her voice growing more strident, her step quickening until Donna wondered if she would have to break into a run to keep up with her.

Finally she came to the death of her husband at night on a busy highway. Their car had slammed over the side; she had been thrown clear, he pinned beneath. No one cared, no one stopped to help; no one in the hundreds tearing past to their own destinations had alerted the highway police.

It had been a great searing sore on her soul, she confessed. She had longed to come home. But when she had finally reached the Manor—

'You found you had brought your habitual thought processes right along with you. No, I am not belittling your right to grief, but this other—we'll go into it later. Meanwhile, hang your nerves around Cupid's neck, and if your sisters think you are slipping, refer them to me. Right?'

Three sisters were at the doors of their suites when they reached that floor. Donna, aware of the ear plugs in her pocket, longed to thrust them at Helena. She didn't dare. She could not foretell what reaction would ensue.

Time now to think of herself? Sultry, her patient confessed as Donna eased her from earlier bandages. She should have her small radio on, check on the possibility of a storm, truly disastrous to the harvest at this time.

And then she looked up, surprised. 'I have been avoiding my radio because of Helena.

Nurse, she turned that off just after you left. Why?'

Donna shrugged, but as soon as possible went to Helena's room to find Helena awaiting her. Quickly then the nurse spoke, handing her the ear plugs on a clean bit of bandage. 'I sterilized them for you.'

Dutifully Helena nodded, preened and seemed to grow in stature. In short, Donna thought, she had achieved personal recognition, and it had been misconstrued as another feather in her cap.

In another moment the radio screamed its protest at being turned on to that volume and Donna, after a quick glance at other doors, a salute to Fanetta, took off on her trip to the highway and Henry Emerson.

For a few moments she basked in the freedom of being able to get into her car and drive away from that House of Hate; immersed her spirit in the glowing beauty of a world golden with harvest, and then in the sight of a slim young man leaning close to his great grain truck, seemingly listening to a radio.

A curve in the road. She looked up, paled, and her gay spirit was blotted out as though by that vast cloud overhead.

CHAPTER SIX

She did not know how long she sat there, the car now silenced. She seemed embalmed in some dreary world from which there was no egress, her only conscious thought that vast peak ahead, blue black at its base but turning grey, then silver, as a cloud swept down from the heavens to embrace it.

'Nurse! Nurse Caffery, Donna!' Henry's voice broke in. 'Are you all right? Something happened back there today, didn't it? You can tell me. Is Mother Jan all right? Which one struck—'

Her attention snapped back to the present.

'I'd better tell you the truth,' she said in a low voice. 'It wasn't the Manor; it was that peak up there wearing a shroud of cloud. No, wait,' as he sought to explain about weather peculiarities in the valley.

'I was engaged to a man in the Air Force for several years. I awakened after he'd left for Viet Nam, realized I didn't and had never loved him. But I hadn't the courage, the nerve, the decency to tell him.'

'There was someone else you'd met?' Somehow he'd sped around the car and was sitting beside her.

'No. No, had there been, I think, at least I hope, I'd have had the courage to speak out.

I didn't. I waited. I waited too long. Oh, I wrote to him often, sent him little things, acted as a waiting fiancée would.

'Then came word he wasn't enlisting for his third stretch and was heading back to me. I thought once we met again, he'd see he no more loved me than I loved him.

'But in his eagerness he chartered a plane in San Francisco and flew up.' She stopped.

'And along the way,' Emerson helped her, 'perhaps over the Siskyous, a storm swept in. Clouds like heavy draperies cut off his view. It's happened to many, Donna; you've read of them. Sometimes whole families—'

'Oh, but don't you understand? Had I been honest, he wouldn't have felt he had to rush back.'

Emerson was silent for a moment. 'I can't quite accept that,' he said. 'You don't know but what he might have reenlisted and been killed over there, or even crossing some busy thoroughfare. Careless driver, that sort of thing—'

Donna smiled ruefully. 'Forgive me. I imagine you have enough problems of your own.'

'That cloud is a forerunner,' he admitted. 'I was checking on the weather report when you drove up. Not good. I'll have the boys work until rainfall tonight, but—' he shrugged—'who knows? That is farming.'

'I won't keep you.' She held out her hand

for the sheaf of mail he carried.

'You're not. Even I need a breather once in a while. How about the house?' He nodded toward the Manor. 'Anything new? They treating you all right?'

'I seem to have made friends of Fanetta and Norah.'

'Norah,' he exclaimed in an unbelieving voice. 'Or for that matter, Fanetta. Of all the screwballs—'

'Oh, please. If she had a shattered leg she could be hospitalized, and, in time, healed, and then learn to use it again. Nerves or nervous conditions are neither so easily identified nor healed. They're so—' she spread her hands out, then glanced up at the descending cloud—'so like that, unpredictable and seemingly impossible to grasp and maneuver into safety.'

'Girl,' he looked at her seriously, 'I've an unhappy feeling I'm going to be confined to the house for a few days. Unhappy because that means the loss of needed money for the women in my life. Ah, but happy if I can spend some of that time with you.'

He jumped out, saluted, turned back and asked her to 'tell the girls I'll be so late for dinner I'll stop in town,' then was on his way.

Donna turned her car and started back, looked up and frowned. Peculiar. That cloud which had shrouded the mountain had either dissipated or moved away. Timing was also an all-important factor in air travel. Well, wasn't it?

'Agreed,' her weary mind replied. 'But had he not been in the air at that particular time—'

She'd switch to the present, to the threatening rain building up just over those mountains, boiling up like steam in a caldron, slopping over. Henry had said this could mean loss of needed money for the women in his life; for the Morgan girls.

Money for what? she wondered, driving on, sharply conscious of the rapid change in the sky overhead. They had shelter, food and, from what he had seen, adequate clothing, though not what she might have chosen.

Or had they been accustomed to so much more any drop in income could set off a cry of poverty?

A final turn in the road, and to the west, north and east the ranch lay spread out. She nodded.

'Taxes,' she mused. 'I wonder what would be left for household use after taxes had been paid from the net profit.'

Perhaps Mrs Montel had lived through such a dour period, and that was why she had had that driving urge to preserve food, to pick and carry, prepare, stand over stoves, fill jars, then hide them away carefully in deep closets. Food against the day there would be little money for such?

But in the Manor? Why not? Oh yes, they could not sell anything. Nor could they dine on objects such as that rococo mirror, its frame so exquisitely carved it was believed to be Chippendale.

Donna went into the rear hall to find four of the women waiting anxiously. Their little gasps, one squeal of glee and one sob, showed the importance of word from the outside to them.

'And Sister Jan?' As one they turned on her.

Tightly Donna's hand clamped the last sheaf, snapped together as the others had been by a rubber band, put there, she was sure, by Henry Emerson.

'I am sure she will share any news with you,' Donna evaded. 'I don't know what is in this.'

Four hands—four claws, she would have said—had been outstretched. Now four voices chanted each would 'run up,' Nurse having had such a busy day.

'But I belong up there,' she murmured. 'I must start preparing her evening meal. Shouldn't you?'

No wonder only Emerson was allowed to pick up mail. Yet why he? Wasn't he Janice Montel's adopted son? He must have established his indifference to their personal lives somehow; made them feel there would be, could be no invasion of their personal privacy.

She trusted she could do the same, though why she wasn't sure. She was there only as Mrs Montel's nurse.

'Hmm,' greeted her patient, stretching eager hands for the mail, 'quite a parcel. Bet my sisters asked to see it. They did, didn't they?'

'What? Oh, Mrs Montel, that newspaper's a coast weekly, isn't it? May I see it after I've prepared your meal? I spent so many vacations down there, not in your area but farther north. That was before Mother died.'

'Then you have no family?'

'One wonderful father, happily married again to a fine companion. But they now live in Alaska.'

There, her attention was diverted. Did her father come down often? He did? And he brought her caribou and moose meat? Wonderful. And furs perhaps?

Now what, wondered the nurse turned dietitian, could she use to complement the thought of wild meat? This was a Vitamin E meal, designed to rebuild scarred tissues. Ah, seasoning.

'Could we risk the balcony?' Mrs Montel asked. 'Even with the fan on, it is so muggy in here. And could you fix a bite to have with me?'

Donna ran down to tell the others and to relay, on request, the contents of the mail: mostly 'get well' cards from former neighbors.

She returned with a tray laden with dishes most of which she wanted to discard and wondered how to do it without the donors being made aware of her rejection.

The balcony was a relief in one sense. There was a breeze building up. There were also clouds over the mountains, cutting off the formidable earlier view.

'Probably no more than a passing shower,' her patient remarked. 'A hot sun tomorrow will bring the grain back to prime.'

Donna could hope for Henry's sake this was true, yet she questioned Mrs Montel's forecast. She believed Henry had heard something more serious on his truck radio.

'My,' her patient breathed, 'you do rate with my sisters. That satin salad is Louella's specialty. Have you talked to her at all?'

'Not really. I chanced to hear her rendition of Schubert's *Unfinished Symphony*. It was so exceptional I had to tell her—'

'Then you are also a musician?'

'No. My mother was a pianist. She was terribly disappointed when she found I could appreciate but not imitate. My fingers were—'

'I understand. There were those who said Louella would make a fine concert pianist, but as Father pointed out, women rarely did. It took a man to give a powerful rendition. At that, whenever she misbehaved or sulked or cried, he'd send her to the piano to, as he called it, "play it out of her system."'

Donna wondered what she had been playing out of her system that day, but asked instead if she had been a mischievous child.

As Mrs Montel took this under consideration Donna tasted the satin salad: jellied sour cream with a piquant flavor. And over here were oriental chicken balls. Astonishing. Now which one had contributed those? Oh, yes, Norah. And what from Helena? What but biscuits as fluffy as the clouds overhead, battered and, beside them, seasoned hard boiled eggs and quince preserves. From Fanetta an apology Donna understood.

Maybe Henry Emerson wasn't doing too badly with these four cooking for him. Nor would she be bothered with disposing of any leftovers. There were none. And her patient approved of her modified diet. It was really a very nice world.

Even the mountains had retreated, thrusting no pyramiding memories into her consciousness. They had earlier. And she had talked, an unusual luxury, this easing the tension with words.

Words. Mrs Montel was talking about Louella, going back to her sister's childhood.

Sneaky, she called her covert acts. Sometimes others paid the price, but when she was proven guilty, 'Father really lit into her.'

'She had a happy marriage?' Donna asked idly. 'She's very attractive.'

Mrs Montel waited a moment, and the wind came in from the southwest, still tinged with a breath of the sea; of conifer-covered mountains, all touched with the acrid scent of fields newly shorn.

Wasn't life like that? thought Donna dreamily. All that happened to one was merged into an undecipherable whole, unless one took time out to isolate, as she did too often and must stop doing.

'Nurse—' The patient's voice lowered, and she gave a quick glance to either side, as though there might be adjoining balconies. But surely the others were below stairs.

'I can talk to you freely. Attractive, you said. She was more than that when young: too pretty, too coy, too enticing. She considered herself in love with a young man Father simply could not accept into the family. He told him so and the young man left, purportedly for some far-away place.

'Then Father found a fine upstanding man, a little older than she, and in time they married. They had the one child. But—most peculiar—the child looked identically like the man Father had sent away. One always wondered if he had returned.'

'A boy then? Where is he now?'

Mrs Montel shrugged. 'Who knows?'

'Barth Borden was killed on a hunting expedition. So many are, you know. He'd left the men he was with, and when he didn't return a search was made. It was deduced some quick-on-the-trigger novice had shot him, thinking he was a deer. It happens so often.'

Donna agreed.

'He was the son?'

'Oh, no, he was the husband, the father. We believe the son is in South America. Mail, we understand, comes to her from there occasionally. She isn't one to talk, you know. Quite close-mouthed.'

She couldn't talk, thought the nurse. Ah, but she had an outlet. She could take her frustration, her grief, her revolt out on the ivories.

'And the other man, the first one, the one she thought she loved?'

'Well, we don't actually know, but we've heard he's been seen around these parts. He's older, no longer handsome. However, he's of no use to Louella. Father stated in his will that, should she ever marry him, she was to be excluded from any benefits of the Morgan estate.'

There was silence. Donna picked up their legged trays, carried them in and swiftly washed the few dishes.

When she returned, the whole world seemed wrapped in a sodden haze that even enveloped her patient.

'Tomorrow will be better,' she cheered the woman. 'There is marked improvement in the calf area, and I believe the veins are down.'

'You'll leave when I can walk again,' protested the woman. 'The quicker I heal, the sooner you'll leave. And, Nurse, I don't know why, but I don't want you to go.'

'Well,' murmured Donna lightly, 'I have a vacation due. If you'll put me up and put up with me, I might enjoy resting here.'

Helping Mrs Montel back into her bedroom, some dreary light having driven them both from the balcony, Mrs Montel remarked the nurse seemed to relate to the family.

'Family,' repeated Donna. 'Do you ever have family reunions?'

'Hardly,' sighed her patient. 'As Father used to say, the less the family saw of the family, the better off they were. That is why none of us really know each other.'

Father! Donna picked up the tray carrying the dishes which had held the sisters' contribution to her dinner. But the thought of their father walked with her. What a life he must have had, accepting as he had the dictum of his father anent the Manor.

As she walked downstairs, she gazed. That original Morgan had not been geographically situated to concentrate upon any one era. Perhaps he used agents. Possibly, too, these gracious furnishings were not authentic.

She had learned quite a bit from an antique dealer whom she had 'home specialed' and realized how difficult it could be to establish the worth of, say, that hoop-backed chair.

Yet because Morgan believed in the intrinsic worth of his accumulation, including the manor house, how many lives had been wrecked?

Which was better: static beauty or peace of mind?

Donna was standing, still holding the tray, gazing into space, when a sound caused her to whirl. Helena had waddled in, an expression of intent determination on her face.

'Ah, you are here,' she remarked; then her chin lifted. 'I don't care what you say; I intend to fix a big sandwich for that boy. So he had dinner in town. By the time he comes in tonight he'll welcome anything.'

She went to her portion of the freezer just outside, well marked, Donna noticed, and from it drew a small package. It proved to contain slices from an earlier roast. These she warmed, then sliced Provelona cheese, the whole topping broad slices of bread. She cut these four ways, trimming off the edges, nibbling these and handing one nibble to Donna.

'Good,' Donna commented, saw a hand go to an ear and raised her voice. 'Delicious. He needs protein. Can he make coffee in his room?'

'You make it here.' Thrusting a thermos at her, Helena started out. 'And leave the sandwich up there. That boy in this weather! My fool son-in-law wouldn't be caught dead in it.'

An hour later a completely bemused Nurse Donna made her laborious way up the steep stairs, wall lights casting a feeble glow on the heavy tray she carried.

A stop for the key to Henry's room, and she went inside. Dreary. These sisters knew this. Yet they had, each in her own way, offered him a welcome home. Gratitude? She wondered.

Swiftly then she worked. That easy chair was drawn to the hearth, a fire laid ready for a match, a small table pulled next to the chair, and on it sandwich, salad, stuffed hard boiled eggs and the thermos of coffee.

She lifted her head. This was rain, not the soft mist for which the area was famous but hard driving rain that would knock down the heads of grain, back the stems, saturate the ground so no equipment could garner any to be sent to a dryer.

Off went the top lights; down bent Donna and lighted the fire.

She swung swiftly. Henry Emerson stood there, his ranch clothes saturated.

'Get out of those immediately,' she ordered in her best professional voice. 'A hot shower is indicated.'

For a long moment he looked at her; then he nodded. 'This rat race may be worth it after all,' he said.

CHAPTER SEVEN

'I—I'll be back,' stammered Donna, heading for the door. 'Ten minutes?' she asked, then added, 'I mean to pick up the dishes and things?'

'Fine. I'll be waiting for you.'

As she closed the door, she looked along the hallway. Four doors. Four heads protruded, anxiety on the faces of each.

'He was pleased,' she reported, 'tired and wet. I'll go back and clean up the tray soon.'

Expressions of satisfaction like sun flicks crossed the worried faces; then each backed into her own suite, and Donna moved on across the hall.

What a travesty of family life, she thought. Here these women were trying, each in her own way, to express concern over the man

76

who was keeping their estate productive, yet so deep was their distrust of each other no one could give him the personal attention he might need.

Then, too, she mused, going on to her patient, their very acts of concern over his welfare were so many thongs tying him to a life he seemed to loathe.

'Been having trouble?' Mrs Montel switched off a television commercial.

'No, I've been thinking,' muttered Donna. 'Oh, you mean I've been below stairs so long?' She reported what had occurred.

'Even if he wasn't hungry,' she explained, 'when one is bone tired, wet and probably cold, the sight of food is recuperative.'

'Cookies,' came the surprising retort. And seeing the nurse's bewilderment, 'That is always my contribution. See that big jar over there? I keep it filled ordinarily. Hank comes in, reaches down and takes a handful to his room to nibble. Store cookies haven't the same flavor, you know.'

'I'll make some boiled cookies in the morning. Oh, they're good.'

'I doubt he'll be going much of any place in the morning except, perhaps, to try to get out any equipment left in the fields. Most peculiar weather. Nurse, I simply must get these legs working. Winter, you know. Must salvage any produce—'

'You develop inner stress, and you won't

salvage anything,' Donna warned.

'Wood,' muttered Mrs Montel. Then, seeing the nurse's look of apprehension, she added, 'Henry can spend the wet time sawing wood for the winter. Oh, he has a chain saw, and heaven knows we still have plenty of small timber he felled during the early spring so it would cure.'

Still Donna waited. Surely they didn't try to heat this mammoth building by fireplace.

'Oh, we have a furnace. It's more than adequate,' Mrs Montel hastened to explain, 'but it is oil. It takes simply hundreds of gallons to heat the area we use here. So costly, we compromise in between seasons by using our hearth-fires.'

Still silent, Donna went about her duties, and Mrs Montel, interpreting her silence as criticism, offered a further defense.

'We each of us,' she stated stiffly, 'have much of considerable worth stored in our suites. We can't afford to have anything mildew.'

Firmly Donna pressed her lips together. Did any of them have anything of more importance than the health and well being of Henry Emerson?

Suddenly remembering him, she completed her duties, checked her wrist watch and, at her patient's anxious demand she 'see to Hank,' went back across the hall.

'Say it out loud,' Emerson ordered when,

78

after answering her door tap, he admitted her.

'You look comfortable,' she evaded.

And he did, in slacks and a colorful sports shirt topped by a warm robe and fleece-lined slippers.

'Comfortable for the first time in the more than three years I've been in this dump.'

'Dump?'

'What else? Break it down to basics.'

Swiftly she did.

'Or do you like this house, admire it?'

'No.' She let the one word suffice. 'Finish your coffee, and if you like I'll run up another thermos full.'

'If you'll join me.' And looking sly, he dug into a chest of drawers to bring out a battered metal coffee maker and a can of the ground commodity. 'Figured this out the first time Mother Jan was in the hospital,' he explained.

Seeming to sense an unexpressed query, he explained, 'I said this atmosphere you created was comforting. Atmosphere takes more than food and a fire; basically, it is an impersonal recognition of another's needs, the needs of a fellow human being. Right?'

She nodded. 'But what puzzles me is why the sisters can't enjoy a central living room, one easily heated in bad weather and—'

'Communal living? Nurse, take five sisters in an area with five television stations.'

Donna laughed. If each chose a different station, there would be battles, and if there were five sets, cacophony.

'Meaning each—' Their glances met and held, and Donna suddenly realized the truth. Each sister considered herself sole heiress of the Morgan menage. To what lengths would they go in their attempt to attain this?

'I mustn't stay,' Donna warned as he began spooning coffee into the container. 'You know—'

'Yes I know,' he agreed. 'But I need to talk to you as a psychiatric nurse and as a girl. How can we arrange it? Any ideas?'

'Planning isn't the solution.' She started toward the door. 'But as we're both alert, the time and place will appear without our manipulation.'

'Agreed. And, Nurse, thank you again. I'll sleep tonight, in spite of that many-thousand-dollar drumming on the roof.'

He might. She didn't. Each sister made an excuse to come calling on her invalid. And each, in an aside, asked Donna what Hank, or Henry, had said. And had she told him anything?

From Helena, 'Did you tell him about Etta coming at me with the poker?'

'Oh, you mean bringing in the fire tong to prove to you it wasn't yours? No, there was no reason.'

From Norah: Had she told Henry about

80

Louella mutilating that beautiful north hedge?

'What north hedge?' Donna responded, knowing full well she had been asking if the nurse had reported one Norah Morgan Norton's reaction to this.

Louella asked only if the nurse had told Henry she approved of her as a pianist.

'We hadn't much time for talking,' evaded Donna. 'I mentioned none of you. But I shall; you should be in a position to spread that beauty outside the walls of the Manor.'

Fanetta was the last to come in, rubbing her hands nervously. 'They're cold,' she explained, and held them to the small hearth in the Montel suite.

It was more than chill, Donna thought, seeing the woman's pallor, her rigidity. A warning glance at Mrs Montel, and she spoke.

'We were about to play a game. Here, will you join us? Or perhaps you'd rather do this in your own suite. It is called *Nothing*.

'That's what it amounts to if we're successful. Wait.' She went to bring out three writing pads and pens.

'Now draw three lines down. Top one with: "Hours wasted on sensations." You know, as in worry, tautness, tremors, all of that type. Really count them by weeks, days, hours. Then at the same time, in the next column, headed: "Result," tabulate what actual effects any of these sensations had on you physically.'

'And the third?' Fanetta asked eagerly.

'Evaluation.'

'That might be interesting. And then?'

'After that, a follow-up game that really takes your mind off the past and present—'

Fanetta waited no longer. She sped out, turned back to smile and say thank you, then hurried on.

Janice Montel sat in thought a moment, then nodded. 'Now with me,' she said, and reached for a pad, 'it will be hours of grueling, grinding work and an estimate of what I or anyone else got out of it. Nurse, listen to that rain thundering down. If one didn't have food stored up—'

'Perhaps your evaluation will show how that food is processed, under duress or enjoyably. I remember the fun my mother used to have. She found tiny half-pints and let me play right alongside her. It wasn't labor; it was a game.'

'A game?' Mrs Montel's voice was rough and deep. 'We were never taught to make games of anything, yet life—'

'I've heard it can be a fun-time if we look at it that way. No, not by neglecting anything. Take sports, golf or tennis. One doesn't neglect perfecting strokes, yet it's fun, or can be.'

And hadn't she better be using this same

therapy on herself? That heavy rain reminded her there had been a bitter storm that fateful night. When contact had been lost with the plane, she had sat tied in knots, seeing Toby injured, drenched.

A little lamely she added, 'Psychiatrists have found if one writes these findings down, after momentary study, the subconscious mind, inner-brain or whatever you want to call it becomes absorbed in the game. It momentarily forgets the physical reactions. And the summation becomes acceptable.'

'But there are those who need it yet would refuse to accept such therapy.'

Donna nodded. 'Usually those who need it the most.'

A moment later, having delivered this judgment she grabbed at a pad, she settled before the fire and began rapidly writing.

Once she paused to add another log to the fire and wondered why this evaluation was so important to her at a time like this. True, she had, a moment before speaking to Emerson at the roadway mailbox, glanced up at that storm-shrouded mountain. This had happened before. Why this fresh new need to clarify her past emotional catastrophe? She'd been living with it for three years, yet now—

Oh, well, how could one teach or aid others without first proving the therapy? And Henry Emerson had said, 'Maybe this rat race is worth it.' Maybe it was. Maybe she could help him realize something from it.

Slightly aghast at what she had found she'd written, Donna paused. A definitely masculine knock had sounded at the hall door.

'Hank,' elucidated Mrs Montel complacently, 'always sounds like he's trying to knock down any obstruction.'

Donna, walking toward the doorway, thought of her first flash at 'Hank'—the fight or flight bit. He would take such direct action as establishing his need to enter.

'This gal gave me a new lease on life.' Emerson came in, preceding her along the wares-laden corridor. 'Had to come in and say thank you for finding her.'

'Finding her!' breathed Mrs Montel. 'My current problem is how to keep her here—long enough,' she added.

'Long enough for what?' he demanded suspiciously.

'To straighten us out, son,' came the reply.

Soberly Emerson turned to Donna. 'We do need it, don't we?' he seemed to muse aloud.

'Who doesn't?' was her honest reply.

'What did she do for you, son?' Mrs Montel queried. 'I mean aside from feeding the inner man?'

'Perhaps that was it,' he replied thoughtfully. 'She fed the real innermost man. I came in from the fields, whipped. You know what I've put into this ranch this year—everything I had to give, hoping maybe—' He seemed to catch himself.

'Hoping maybe,' Mrs Montel offered, 'there'd be enough left over to see us through any lean years?'

It wasn't, thought Donna, what he'd really meant, yet he nodded.

'Then this, something over which neither I nor any other grain grower has any control. If it keeps up—'

The three paused. A steady, deadly thrumming of rain struck the balcony roof even as it had been striking it now for hours.

'Perhaps Nurse should teach you how to play a new game,' Mrs Montel comforted him: 'writing down what we worried about five, ten years ago and finding out how unimportant it seems now.'

'Because this is more devastating by comparison?' he asked.

'No,' she flashed 'rather, because we become aware of what such negative emotions as worry can do to us physically: literally pour poison into our systems.'

'Mental or physical poison?' he quipped.

'Both,' she returned. 'If you're interested, I will send for the latest findings on the physical side confirming the body's swift response to emotional stress. Even the most reactionary medical men are now making this concession.'

'And the cure?'

'It really depends upon the individual. As I don't know you very well—'

'Ah,' a great smile encompassed her, 'we'll take care of that. Mother Jan, will you brief your sisters on this? Nurse Caffery is giving me psychiatric treatment; hence we need to be alone together frequently.'

Donna debated throwing something at him; then she laughed. 'After that comeback, I doubt you need any help from anyone.'

'Well—' he rose, stretched—'this I have to sleep off. Something tells me I'm going to need nerve strength piled up in my inside bank. Going to have to draw on it if dawn doesn't ride in on the sun.'

Dawn rode in on heavy clouds, intermittent showers and general gloom. But Henry Emerson did not appear at the breakfast table. He'd already driven off from the home grounds.

Yet the meal was not without interest. Fanetta appeared and was promptly draped with adjectives. She looked kittenish, pert, perky, as though she had something up her sleeve.

And with each remark the inner glow seemed to dim, a vague cloud of uncertainty shadow the early happiness of her mien.

'Do you always dissect each other at breakfast?' Donna dared ask.

Norah voiced the feeling of the others. How anyone, especially a Morgan, dared look happy after a night like last night; dared look forward to a day with no promise of fair weather! It meant to each of the others she really did have 'something up her sleeve.'

Donna smiled at Fanetta. 'If that sleeve isn't too raveled, would you like to drive into town with me for supplies? Oh, sorry,' she told the sudden clamor. 'I've room for only one. Another time?'

She confided in her patient. She needed material to provide supplies for that cookie jar. What did Mr Emerson prefer? Butterscotch, chocolate or vanilla? Nuts or raisins or both? And was there anything she, Mrs Montel, wanted?

'Crossword puzzles. A recess for the mind,' she told the puzzled nurse. 'Pick the easy ones; the others make me mad. But with the easy ones, five, ten, fifteen minutes at a time, I can give my worries a rest.'

As for flavors, Henry enjoyed each and every one.

In the car, heading out along slick roads, mist-ridden hills, ghostly stands of trees, Fanetta sat silent until Donna challenged her.

'I did feel wonderful until they started in on me.'

'Hmmm.' Donna negotiated a flooded curve where a brimming stream sought to inundate the small bridge. 'I'd figured you as a fighter. But then too few people recognize the need to fight for their freedom from fear, from nerves, from distress.

'Would you sit silently, or tied up in tendon knots, and let others, even sisters, pile their own insecurities, their fears, their woes upon you?'

'Certainly not.'

And then, ten miles later, she said, 'Oh, but I did, even after that written run-down which told me so much about my own reactions to living. It was a coward's reaction.'

When she drove back to Morgan Manor she found three sisters in the carport awaiting her. She heard one remark, 'She didn't lie. The back of her car is loaded.'

It was. It held a great roll of foam rubber which, once spread across the doubtful comfort of the Morgan double bed in the Montel suite, would afford her patient greater ease.

They noted, too, that Fanetta had regained the euphoric appearance she'd had that morning.

Instantly they charged. Had she had the car radio on? She hadn't? Then she hadn't heard the weather report?

'Continued heavy showers,' charged Norah Norton, as though Nurse Caffery were brewing them up in some hidden recess. 'Do you know what that means to us?'

'You have food. You have shelter,' Donna began.

'Come on; lunch is waiting. But you should know the truth about what Henry has done to us.'

CHAPTER EIGHT

Nurse Donna Maria Caffery checked first on her patient. She was improving rapidly. Actually, she did not need a special. An aide, could they find one who would remain, would suffice. Or a sister.

Yet what sister would Henry Emerson trust after the balcony railing episode? Perhaps the extra money going into her wages meant more to his peace of mind than the actual cash in the bank.

How ridiculous! Or was it? There had been Fanetta, truly a nice person, striding toward her sister, iron tong in hand, ready to bring it down on that sister's head rather than on the radio, had Helena stepped between Fanetta and the set. And Norah with those hands curved to choke. No, Henry was not wrong in assuming he needed safe, impersonal care for the woman who had cared for him as a small boy when his world had capsized.

No wonder none of the younger members had remained at the Manor. Had they a better sense of values? Perhaps. Perhaps they had felt the silent warfare was not worth the purely fortuitous chance of inheriting.

Mrs Montel had turned her television to the noon news. A most bewildered so-called weatherman was attempting to explain the strange course of air patterns.

This was August. It didn't rain in August. Yet the skies were weeping convulsively. And there was no indication they would dry their tears, beam out sunshine and try to recoup the losses they had inflicted upon the tiny human of the species who were attempting to grow food to keep their kind in existence.

Swiftly Donna assembled the food, most of which she had picked up, prepared, in town, then bed tray at the ready, waited for dismissal.

'Run down and have your lunch,' ordered her patient, 'and don't miss a word the girls are saying. I want to know everything.'

Perversely, at least in the beginning, the sisters were more interested in the foam rubber than in the weather. True, Norah admitted heavily, Manor beds had been purchased before anything but coils and beauty of covering were considered.

'Personally,' she said gloomily, 'I arise each morning marked by a coil. Would this foam thing you bought offset that!'

'Frankly—' this was one of Helena's hearing days—'that was why I fought so to have my own—that is, my married—that is, the bed I myself bought—put up. But you, Norah, were the first of those who refused me that comfort.'

'Maybe—' Louella looked slyly from one to the other—'the day will come when we awaken to what we've burdened ourselves with.'

'Burdened!' For once there was unity.

'And just where or how, with your limited income,' Norah asked loftily, 'could you provide yourself with a grand piano such as the one you use to keep us awake?'

'Oh?' Louella retorted brightly. 'And I thought that was Helena's radio, or television, whichever she chances to have on, that kept us all awake. Wasn't it?'

And Helena was suddenly unable to hear. 'What did she say?' she asked first one, then another.

'Foam rubber.' Donna spoke directly at, not to her, seeking to ease the atmosphere.

'How much?' came in unison.

When she reported the cost, a deep silence fell on those at the table.

'We can't, any of us, afford one *this* year,' stated Norah. She held up her hand, and all listened to that beat of the rain.

Donna thought of the row crops that had

gone to freezers and canneries, and as though reading her mind, one and then another sought to explain.

Taxes came first. For some 'insane' reason, the state had decided to tax such land as theirs as a potential building area. And taxes had to be paid.

'Then,' Norah sighed, 'with me at least, there is insurance—hospitalization, accident. Oh, surely you as a nurse know the many claims insurance makes upon us? I am still driving; so is Louella. We both have our yearly car insurance payments to meet. And with no income but that from the farm—'

Poor Henry, thought Donna. Then her mind switched to her patient. Here was one of her reasons for driving herself to provide such food as she could preserve. Had they gone through years of need before? And in the good years, hadn't there been enough to see them through the others?

Yet Henry Emerson had been at the Morgan Manor only three years. Hmm, interesting.

Slightly disturbed, Donna started for Mrs Montel's suite, wondering how much she dared breathe of what had been said.

Dutifully she reported the sisters' interest in the foam mattress lining. Pressed, she reported they seemed concerned about meeting personal obligations, such as insurance payments.

'We had one horrible year,' Mrs Montel offered, 'the one before Henry took over. The man running the ranch did everything wrong, and we came out literally cleaned of cash.

'If Henry hadn't loaned my sisters the money, their policies would have lapsed. And had I and the others not processed food, we could have had a lean winter.'

What price a manor house, wondered Donna, then took it further. Could any of these women have made enough, through personal labor or ability, to have met these expenses plus food and lodging?

'Oh,' she said aloud, but refused to reveal what her mind had suddenly presented.

'Henry's cookies,' Donna evaded Mrs Montel's query, and promptly set about a labor of love.

Mrs Montel watched dubiously as Donna worked boiling sugar and milk and butter, then switching the tall pot away and adding quick cooking oats, peanut butter and seasoning.

Chopped cashew nuts and raisins, and where on earth in the suite could she find room to stretch the length of waxed paper to accept the spoonfuls of dough?

'Take that cover from that elbow-high stack,' ordered the now fascinated patient. 'Just china-ware and silver packed in those cartons. They wash.'

Dabs dropped, crisscrossed by a fork; then a few were tucked into the tiny refrigerator. A few moments later Donna presented these to Mrs Montel.

'Why, these are good,' she exclaimed. 'They are even delicious.'

Ah, another crisis passed! Donna, clearing up the area of her activities, wondered what would happen next.

A rap at the door. Louella sidled in and tried to converse with the nurse by raised eyebrow.

After her brief conference with her sister, mostly about the weather, Louella left, and Donna followed.

'That game you taught Fanetta,' Louella said urgently. 'Please, please teach it to me.'

For a moment Donna waited, then spoke softly. 'I am told your father used to send you to the piano to play off your troubles.'

Louella shrugged.

'Have you ever tried composing?'

'Composing? Me?' came in surprise. Then, after a moment, 'Well, I did have one stretch of playing in public at a small theater. And people did come down and ask what I'd been playing. I could never answer. I had been improvising.'

'Improvising your feeling toward your life; toward the Manor; toward the goal you would like to reach.'

For a long moment the grey-blue eyes held

94

Donna's gaze; then a sob sounded. 'And I didn't want you here,' she said. 'I was willing to do almost anything to keep any nurse—'

'Go take that out on the ivories immediately,' Donna ordered. 'Quickly, before you lose that emotion.' And Louella fled.

'What did she want?' demanded Mrs Montel. 'What did she say? What did you tell her?'

'Oh,' Donna shrugged, 'Fanetta seemed so much better this morning, Louella wanted to know what I'd done for her. So I told her—well, sort of—'

'Sort of. My goodness, Nurse, Louella has never taken a directive from anyone. She slips and slides.'

'Why?' Donna cut in innocently.

Mrs Montel started to answer, then dropped her head. 'Nurse—' her voice was a whisper—'I never before tried to understand the why of it. Louella is the youngest, the one most likely eventually to become heiress of the Manor. None of us ever thought beyond that.

'And now I am seeing her as a child, a baby—a motherless baby, for our mother died at her birth, and we chose to blame that tiny mite.

'We hated her,' she added slowly. Then her defenses reared. 'But she was so—well, so sly and sneaky and—'

95

Donna waited.

'All right,' Mrs Montel muttered; 'now I understand why. The only way she could hold her own with us older, stronger ones was to slip in, unobserved, and act before we were alerted and could stop her.'

Poor Louella, thought Donna. In the beginning she had been cheated of loving care because in their willful ignorance the others had blamed her for their mother's death. Then later, as the youngest, she became their greatest threat to inheriting the Manor.

And when in desperation she sought love, her father checked that, didn't he? She posed the question.

'I suppose, though Borden seemed a fine man. Solid, you know.'

'Then why, on his death, was she left destitute, if she were?' Donna asked, remembering the tongue lashing Louella had received when she dared suggest the Manor could be a burden.

'We never fully understood. And of course his death was never really explained. It was presumed a hunting accident, yet the court—'

'Then there was some evidence of—' Donna chose not to use the word murder, nor even willful killing.

'Nurse, what is that terrible noise?' Mrs Montel's voice arose to a new high.

Donna turned, listened, then sped out of the suite and down the stairs.

Louella had taken her advice, but she had failed to close the great doors. And now the fury, the desperation, and that futility of her life were being pelted in discordant sounds at the Manor walls. Aaron Copland would have said Louella, as composer, was in violent contact with *la matière sonore*, unaware of anything but the reverberation of sound within her mind or soul and her need to disperse it.

Swiftly Donna worked, sliding the great doors from areas where they seemed to have become fixed, first in the front parlor, then in the back parlor, finally in the living room. Only then, after swinging those between each room further to condense sound, did she move to the music room.

As she sealed those closing off the foyer, three sisters met her in a phalanx.

'Those doors,' Norah informed her, 'have not been closed since Father died.'

'Father,' Fanetta's voice was shrill, 'believed everything should be kept in the open.'

'That noise was so dreadful—' began Helena.

'Imagine you noticing.' Donna smiled sweetly. 'And Fanetta, the Nothing game can be played without paper. Mrs Norton—' she turned to the latter—'would it not ease

Mrs Montel's son if heat were kept within smaller areas? Now, if you will excuse me—'

As one the three stood; then Helena, who had registered every word, every inflection, turned. 'No one has ever dared talk to us like that.'

'I wonder how far she would really go,' Fanetta mused thoughtfully.

'We can demand another nurse,' Norah stated, 'after I have my arthritis under control, naturally.'

Back in the shadows of a side entrance, Henry Emerson stood silent. He had problems enough and to spare. Now this.

A fresh storm swept in, struck with such force even the heavy walls and ceilings of the Manor could not dim its drenching fury.

All right, then, he would fight. Someone had to do something to check the equally heavy downpour of envy, hatred, avarice, jealousy, and above all fear that deluged this edifice with poisoned emotions, seeped into the individuals to manifest itself in physical disease and disorder.

The Manor was quiet the rest of that afternoon. Henry had said he would bring in the mail. He did, and Donna went down to pick up her patient's share, if any.

All heard Louella's choking sob as she thumbed through hers, then saw her turn and flick away, hurrying, the nurse assumed, to her suite.

'South America?' demanded Norah.

Emerson shook his head. 'I wouldn't know. I arranged with the post office to do the sorting.'

Louella was forgotten abruptly. Helena had glanced at her own mail and wailed, and Norah, with one look at a letter she had opened, cried, 'Do those idiots think we are made of money? All they need, they say, is a thousand—'

'Thousand?' Helena was hearing very well. 'Mine demanded five thousand.'

Fanetta said nothing, but her thin hands curled claw-like, crumpling a letter she held.

Only her patient read her mail with complacency. But then, Donna reasoned, her only child, adopted though he was, was on the giving, not the receiving end.

There was quite a bustle in the kitchen before dinner. The nurse in Donna evaluated it. Norah and Helena were building mountains of food; Fanetta recoiled but attempted to keep up with their apparent interest in the evening meal. Louella didn't appear.

Of course, thought Donna, this is their only creative activity. How did they stand being closed in between these dour walls with nothing to do, really, nothing to which to look forward except the death of the others which would free them to live in a wider, brighter world? What a life! No wonder they indulged in hospitalization at the drop of a diagnosis. Anything was better than this.

Henry gravely thanked Donna for the 'so-called boiled cookies,' complimenting her. Promptly she ran up for samples, then was questioned on how they were made and educated on the various improvements each would employ in her own preparation.

Come talk of crops and the selling thereof, and when he admitted he had sold there came a wail of despair.

'In this weather? With so many hundreds of acres ruined? The price is bound to go up.'

'It could,' he admitted. 'But meanwhile, so would the insurance and holding fees, possibly offsetting any increase.'

Well, if each had her way, things would be handled differently.

'I'll be happy to turn it over to you at any time,' Emerson told them.

'In a year like this!' they scoffed. 'And,' contributed Norah, 'I noticed you left equipment on that southwest ninety.'

'Even as Carlton has left his on his east one thousand,' agreed Emerson, and did not know it would continue to stand there, bogged down, for months.

Donna looked across and longed to take him in her arms, to give him reassurance. And all she could offer was foolish cookies.

'Henry,' Norah posed a new threat, 'is there any reason we can not borrow on the crop? I mean with this Manor as collateral—'

'For how long would that collateral remain only that? What would be the value of the dollar by the time the remaining heir might sell?' he asked reasonably. 'Surely you've paid out enough in attorney's fees to know the validity of the Morgan will.'

And silence as dark and heavy as the evening fell.

Why did he put up with such a life? Donna wondered. He needn't. He could find pleasurable employment and contribute Mrs Montel's living expenses. Why? Was it a challenge, or what?

Mrs Montel placed a few questions. How had Louella acted after her musical purgative? She hadn't come in to dinner? Nurse must check on her immediately; that was completely out of character.

Louella's door stood open. When she didn't answer to Donna's knock, the nurse walked in. Louella had obviously dined in her suite and dined well. A book of popular jokes lay face down on the table.

Could she have had a happy time for a change?

A soft wind whisked down the chimney, lifted flakes of half burned letters from the fireless hearth.

Donna noticed this, turned to walk away

and then stood frozen.

A shot had rung out below, and following the shot a scream, a woman's scream that rose, then stopped abruptly.

CHAPTER NINE

Now came an echoing scream from Mrs Montel, her voice calling desperately, 'Nurse, Nurse, quickly!'

Her duty lay there, surely, yet thoughts like swift films shot across the eyes of her professional mind. Someone had been harmed, perhaps fatally. She would know. Perhaps she alone could offer the only sane aid.

A second shot glazed the window of Louella's suite, and Donna went into action, turning lights off then speeding to Mrs Montel's suite, touching a switch to that illumination, ordering the bed lamp off until the blinds could be closed.

Below stairs voices were raised in terror. Finally, glancing out through a hall window, Donna saw the grounds of the Morgan mansion ablaze with outdoor lights, deftly placed.

Henry Emerson, rifle in hand, was slinking along a hedge. It couldn't have been he. Well, could it? That had been a rifle shot, and that was what he was carrying.

'It's Louella,' cried Norah, as Donna sped down the stairs. 'Do something quickly, Nurse; do something. Here—'

A cape was thrown over her shoulders, and without further thought Donna rushed out toward Henry, in the general direction from which the shot and the cry had sounded.

Henry whirled as she neared. 'Get back in there,' he rapped. 'Turn off those damned lights.'

'Not till I've checked her.'

'If you live that long. Donna, the lights—I've a flash here.'

If she lived that long? Ah, both would be 'sitting ducks' if the one firing were still in that outer darkness. A flash would give the rifleman a minimal target.

She called the order, half explaining and darkness came down like a weight. She stumbled ahead as it suddenly blotted out the terrain.

'Here.' Henry half fell, then turned to aid Donna's approach to the prone figure of Louella.

Swiftly she knelt, told Henry how to play the flashlight, but refused to answer questions.

'I'll stay; you call an ambulance,' she ordered.

'I can't leave you here,' he groaned.

'Hank, get an ambulance quickly, and then the sheriff's office.'

She had been alone with approaching death before but never under circumstances such as these. And she had to fend off that death if it were within her power. Poor little Louella.

Even as she sought to pinpoint the spot where the bullet had entered, the figure stirred.

'Louella,' she said softly, 'this is Nurse Donna. You had a slight accident. Do you mind lying very still?'

'For you,' came the faint whisper. A moment later, 'He hates me so.'

'Who hates you?' Then the nurse regretted the question, for the head rolled. 'Not now; ease down. *Lento*,' she added, and the body relaxed.

There came the sound of another shot, and perversely, Donna relaxed. This was far away, back to the southwest where a dirt road meandered over low lying hills. But the timber had had the same reverberation, and she believed the one originally shooting was offering a farewell.

Henry came from that direction. Yes, he'd called. The ambulance was on its way, as was the sheriff. Then he began questioning Donna closely until she signaled for silence. Louella was becoming restless. If they wanted to save her—

'You didn't—' His question seemed a charge of negligence as he stared at the sodden shoulder.

'No. There was coagulation. Not safe to chance disruption without additional help at hand.' And then they lifted their heads at the far-away cry of a siren.

'You will go in with her—'

'And Mrs Montel—'

'Believe me, Nurse, I shall sleep in that suite with this at hand, or one like it. Ah, I'll meet them.' And he was off, heading for the main driveway.

Later, much later, Donna would review those many moments, the instinctive gestures as she removed the cape thrown over her and Hank stripped his heavy jacket, the latter going around Louella's feet, the cape across the rapidly rain-soaking body.

Yet at the time it seemed all were condensed within a capsule labeled Time.

Men came with a guerney, accompanied by an intern, and swiftly Donna reported her findings. 'Smart girl,' approved the intern. 'You could have—'

'I know,' she agreed.

As the trained men moved Louella to the guerney, thence to the ambulance, Donna raced for dry clothing to carry with her. Then they were on their way, her mind carrying the sharp etching of three terrified sisters clustered at the top of the stairway.

105

The ride seemed endless, though it was not more than thirty odd miles. Louella regained consciousness, and her gaze sought and held that of Donna.

The intern moved back, and Donna sat beside her in cozy intimacy.

'I,' Louella whispered, 'was shot.'

'Probably some early hunter mistook your flashlight for the eyes of wild life. We'll run you in and check on the wound. Then—fun—I'll sit it out with you at home. Agreed?'

'You won't leave me?' came in the faintest voice.

'Except for a few minutes. I need fresh duds. I'm all sprinkled down, if you notice.' She talked on softly, and Louella's eyes closed, her breathing became even.

Outside emergency, Donna waited until an orderly came out. 'They removed the bullet, are holding it for the sheriff. She seems to have ridden this out okay. Doc wants to know if you can stand the night duty.'

'Will do,' Donna agreed.

'Patient kept saying you'd understand. By the way, deputy in admittance is waiting to talk to you.'

So was Dr Michael, who came out to frown at Donna, then nod. He'd checked her out with Haskell.

'Haskell said he hadn't wanted you sent to

that House of Hate. Know what he meant?'

'I do now,' the nurse reported ruefully. 'Yet someone has to be there, so why not me?'

'After this?'

'I'm not sure yet what happened, especially not why. Mrs Borden has a habit of wandering outside at night, flashlight in hand.'

'On nights when rain is pouring as it is tonight? Look, nurse, track that down. Track down her reason for going out other nights, alone. Run a test on it; then let me know if you come up with the same theory as the one I've reached.'

Donna bowed her head in thought. Louella had said, there at the beginning, 'He shot me.' And later, 'He hates me so.' How identify the one called he? But that was the duty of the sheriff's men.

She thought then of the shreds of paper in the fireplace. Could the evening wanderings have been to meet someone out of her past? Who? What about the son? But he wouldn't; surely not. His father had been shot while hunting, hadn't he? Yet there had been no posthumous settling of the estate.

Alerted, Donna went in to glance quickly at Louella, still under an anesthetic, nod to the nurse and, at a signal from the doorway, go on to face a sheriff's deputy.

What would she tell him? The time,

naturally; one did glance at one's wrist watch. Then about the second shot grazing the window.

After a moment's silence the deputy smiled. 'Nurse, come clean. Which is better in the long run—honoring your patient's confidence or protecting the rest of the people at the Manor? For that matter, protecting her from another, possibly fatal shot?'

A deep sigh came from Donna. 'Thank you. Actually, I know nothing of immediate value. Call it, rather, woman's intuition. When I reached her she made two remarks. One, "He shot me." The other, "He hates me so."'

'From that I assume she knew who it was.' After a moment's thought, remembering what Dr Michael had said, 'Perhaps she had met him out there in the dark garden before. Perhaps she had arranged to meet him tonight. I don't know, but neither do I know that she knew who had shot at her. It could have been a third party. She may have assumed it was the other.'

'And you have no idea—' He let it ride. After a moment he challenged, 'You had a thought. Why not try it out on me?'

Donna shook her head as though to free it of fancies. 'The family would know better than I. Oh, all right. I remembered my patient telling me the man Mrs Borden had loved when she was young and whom her father wouldn't let her marry had been, she called it "seen around these parts."'

'Good!' He snapped his notebook shut and stood up. 'Now we have something to work on. I'll contact the family. Maybe nothing will come of it, but it's better than sitting by while some wild guy with a gun in hand runs loose.'

He left, and she went to the corridor. There was still a little while until she went on duty. Coffee was indicated and, checking, she learned where to find the cafeteria, then made her way there.

She had coffee. She also had a pat on the shoulder when Dr Michael came in.

'Nice work, Nurse. Sometimes it's a bit difficult for us to remember our basic duty is saving, not risking lives. Sure you feel up to this next stretch of duty? Have another standing by, but the patient seems to relate to you. She'll probably come out of anesthesia and into a nightmare world. You can dispel those shadows if anyone can.'

Shadows. Later, bending low to catch the words Louella murmured, Donna wondered if she too were in that world.

'So he killed you,' were the first words. Then a bewildered, 'We are dead, aren't we?'

She could ask who had killed them, but somehow it seemed more important for a nurse to carry a patient across the thin line.

'No, dear. You had a little accident. You wanted me to care for you. I am. I'm right here beside you in a hospital.'

'Hospit-al. Not,' the voice faltered, then breathed, 'the Manor?'

'No, a big, strong building full of fast stepping doctors, nurses and orderlies. And my, do they have to trot to keep up with things. Why not have a good rest?'

'Rest. Yes, here.' She seemed to melt back into the bed, then stiffened. 'You won't go away?'

'Not until you wake up and tell me to bring you some breakfast.'

'Ah.' And Louella Borden slipped away into the haven of natural sleep.

Donna sat in the window, low lights behind her. Below and beyond, hundreds, thousands of lights polka-dotted the night. Beautiful, who wanted to live in the lonely, dark Manor?

Swiftly her mind spanned the distance. Thank goodness she had changed that dressing. Had she not, it could have dried in the still suppurating area, pulled and given fresh distress to Mrs Montel.

In the morning she would be returning to the Manor. How? Her car was there. Well, morning would take care of that. But imagine having to remain on after this night of horror. She must. Somehow she must, or the fear of the others would be even greater than it must be now.

She thought of Henry growing more lean, more taut. How, why did he stand this? He had the potential for a much more rewarding life.

All right, she scoffed, why are you returning without protest?

She thought that morning would never come; then suddenly it was there. Physician, surgical nurse, others had come in to check during the dark hours, and now here was her relief. Louella was still sleeping. Nor had she, Donna, yet decided what kind of transportation she would find to return her to her other duty.

'I'll run down and have breakfast,' she told the relief. 'If she wakens, tell her I'm still here. She has—oh, call it a thing about me being around just now. She'll get over it quickly enough.'

Donna chose her breakfast with an eye to nutrition rather than appetite. Yet it was good to be back in a familiar atmosphere.

She carried her tray to a small table, sat down, then looked up. Henry Emerson had just entered. Now he stood scanning the tables, a Henry so lean, so brittle Donna believed he would splinter at a sharp sound.

Slowly she stood up, and he strode toward her, her regulation cape streaming back from his arm.

'Sit down,' she ordered.

'Have to get back.'

'Isn't there someone there?'

'Yes, they left a deputy. Fine fellow, but—'

'Sit down,' she ordered, 'I need my breakfast. So do you. Now while I pick up something for you, *let go!*'

'Let go? Oh, oh—well, yes.' And he laid her cape on a chair, sat down, started to rise, smiled grimly and saluted. 'I'm letting go,' he assured her.

For a man in his state, hot cakes lush with butter and syrup and, slyly, alongside these bacon and eggs. Family fare. And with it a toast to a night saved from tragedy in fruit juice.

'Now eat or I'll be embarrassed,' Donna warned him. 'And between bites tell me how everything is at the Manor. Mrs Montel?'

'Ridiculous.' He looked up, fork well laden. 'She seems to be taking this better than the rest. Says if you are in command—'

'Command? Me?' Donna laughed. 'Anything but. I am sort of a wastebasket into which people throw even valuables because they don't realize what they're tossing away.'

'Whatever you picked up out of that basket is good, I understand. They haven't let me in on it, but I understand the sheriff has a so-called "lead." ' For some reason he checked with Mom Jan. Any ideas?'

Donna winced. 'Full of them, but none make sense. Good hot cakes, aren't they? How is she feeling this morning?'

'Sounds idiotic, but she seems brighter, better. Don't get it. The other three are frozen with fear.'

He talked then. Questioned, he related the reaction of each. Fanetta showed deep depression. Norah said, Well, I've taken other things; I'll brace myself to this. Only Helena seemed shaken by hysteria.

Donna looked up to see a boy, coffee maker in hand, and nodded. Swiftly he filled their cups, and she smiled her gratitude. Their story had obviously reached the staff.

Suddenly Henry's elbow went to the table; his head rested upon his hand. 'Donna, have you any idea what it means to me to be able to talk like this? Talk freely and not be afraid I'm letting "any of the girls" down?'

'I do, Hank,' she replied softly. Hadn't she been in desperate need to talk to someone? And there was no one anywhere to whom she could relate the inner agony of her grief.

It was then a signal came. 'Have more coffee,' she advised. 'Louella is awake and wants me. You have time to wait?'

'No one,' he stated, 'is more important to me than you.'

She wasn't gone too long, but it must have seemed eons to Henry. He was waiting in the lounge and swiftly came to her, aware of some change.

'Something wrong? She's worse?'

'No,' Donna could reassure him; 'she's out of danger. She's been moved from intensive care to a private room.' And then she wondered who would underwrite the time ahead and wondered how soon she might relieve Henry, if Louella could and would be returned to the Manor.

'Come on,' she added, let him drape her cape, and they went down to his car.

'It's devilish foggy outside,' he warned as they started.

It was, and as they progressed from city to country roads, the fog thickened until driving became a dangerous challenge. Yet, perversely, there was always a short span ahead where visibility was clear.

'Rather like life, isn't it?' Donna mused. 'You look at it as a whole and wonder how you can possibly make your way through. But if you take it a mile or even quarter-mile or a few hundred feet at a time, you progress.'

'And when you look back,' he picked up her thought, 'you wonder why you worried over the whole trip when you could only travel a wheel round at a time.'

They had moved slowly on for many miles when he spoke again. 'Louella has told you something. I need not know. But how does she feel about "getting it off her chest"?'

'Like someone who's lived under a sharp sword hanging by a thread for twenty-odd years. It's finally fallen and only nicked her in passing. Oh, isn't this the—'

'Yes, and that's the deputy coming down the road at a trot. Oh, man, now what?'

CHAPTER TEN

Henry speeded, then slowed to a stop as the deputy sheriff came alongside.

'They've picked him up,' he reported, 'picked up Jim Crake, Louella's Crake—that is, Borden's husband. He's confessed, not just to trying to do her in but to murdering Borden.'

The car had stopped. Donna moved over as the deputy moved in beside her. 'Thanks to you,' he added.

'To me?' Donna asked, for what had she known before this last talk with Louella?

'Yeah. He'd holed in out there way beyond the boundaries of the Morgan place. Built him a small cave, complete with covers, dishes, food. The only thing he'd run out of was money. When Mrs Crake, that is Borden, ran out of that, he figured he'd had it. So he took action. Said if he did her in, then, as her legal husband, he'd be set for some benefits.'

'And he didn't know he was no longer her legal husband?' Donna asked. 'Oh, I understand. I didn't know until about an hour ago.'

Henry remained silent for a moment, then straightened. 'I think this is something to be talked out before the whole family,' he stated. 'If we don't—' He let their minds pick up the possibilities.

The car moved on, and where before there had been dense fog, there seemed to be an opening allowing the Morgan mansion to stand out, starkly magnificent against its gray background.

Donna gave it one look. What hostility had been brewed within those walls, what suffering. If one admitted Louella's father had been right in his earlier evaluation, why had he not followed through? And Louella's son?

Normally 'the girls' came beyond the doorway to greet anticipated visitors or returnees. Not today. They huddled in the upperhall, hands on doors that could be swiftly locked.

'You are all safe,' Henry called up to them. 'Jim Crake has been captured.' He waited for their voiced wonder to quiet. 'He's admitted firing the shot. He's also admitted it was he who murdered Borden. He'll be behind bars for the rest of his life.'

'Now—' they were moving up the stairway—'give Nurse a chance to check on Mother; then we'll all meet in there. I'll call you when we're ready.'

'I'll make coffee,' came the astounding reception of the news from Norah. 'Girls, will you give me a hand?'

In the Montel suite Emerson hesitated. 'This is going to be, for women of their generation, woman-talk, isn't it?'

Imagine him recognizing the generation gap in communications. 'It is.' Donna nodded. 'But stand by. I'm not sure how each will take it. I might need help.'

'Will do. And, Donna—' he held her elbows and looked down at her—'I don't know what I've done to deserve you. At a time like this—' He loosened his grip and threw wide his arms. 'Call me when you need me.'

Moving on through the tight space, a slim avenue lined with cartoned, boxed and trunked belongings, Donna faced her patient.

'Oh, Nurse, you're here. Sister? They said she was out of danger. Is she?'

'Insofar as anyone can tell at a time like this, yes. Now let's take a peek at those pedal extremities of yours.'

'They ached so during the night.'

'Naturally. You were willing them to run; putting pressure on them.'

117

'Why, I was, I really was. But I wasn't aware of what I was doing to myself.'

'One seldom is.' Donna stopped short, gazing at the gory inner swabs. Mrs Montel was going to need a check-up immediately.

Swiftly she cleansed, applied a needed antibiotic and new dressings and thought: Truly this is the poison exuded by this Morgan mansion.

She talked a little. Mrs Montel knew, didn't she, that she had nothing to fear? She was not trapped with a maniac roaming the Morgan grounds. The man was captured, had confessed and would be incarcerated for many years if not for his entire lifetime.

Ah, her words had done more than the emollient. Muscles relaxed and the legs eased down, lay flat, inert.

A mild sedative; then Donna spoke again. Yes, she would rest, but first she must talk to all of the Morgan girls, perhaps clarify suspicions they had carried for years. Louella, she told Mrs Montel, had talked freely.

Talked, Donna would have said, as though she had been given some verbal laxative which had released the agonies of untold days and years.

The sisters came in a little suspiciously. They sat on straight-backed chairs and focused on this nurse who had come into their life.

'Louella,' Donna went immediately to the subject, 'asked me to tell you the truth, the entire truth. You may not approve, but is there anyone anywhere who doesn't have some deep secret that could be healed by airing it?'

'What did she say?' Helena began to chant. 'Tell me, Etta, what she's saying?'

Donna smiled at her, went over, pulled the ear plugs and suggested she try using her ears normally for a change.

And then she talked, briefing them on what Louella had told her, clipping from it the agony, the remorse, giving the outline tersely and inadvertently laying the blame where she inwardly felt it lay.

They all remembered, she told them, their sister Louella's infatuation for a young man named James Crake. Judging from the response, they did.

And their father's reaction? He had sent Louella away to an adjoining state, purportedly because he believed she had incipient tuberculosis. Ah, but did they know Louella had gotten in touch with Crake and that he had joined her there and that there had been a secret marriage, easily accomplished in that state in those days?

Shock, contempt, wonder and complacent remarks came from the four.

Then Mr Morgan had insisted Louella marry Borden. She told her father the truth,

119

and he attempted to have the early marriage invalidated. He thought he had. It didn't hold when Crake contested, but meanwhile Louella had married Borden, unable to stand up to her father and realizing there was a child on the way.

Borden had been a decent fellow, considerably older than Louella. By the time he was told of the early marriage, the son, Braden Borden was two years old and Barth Borden was delighted with him, despite the fact the baby was not his own.

But he couldn't without bringing dishonor upon his wife, make a legal adoption. And he believed what Morgan had told him: that the earlier marriage was legally dissolved.

'And Louella?' urged the sisters. 'Why didn't she do something? Why didn't she—'

'Which of you stood up against your father's dictates?' Donna asked. 'And if you had a child you adored, would you subject him to disgrace by unearthing the truth?'

So Louella had lived with this fear of disgrace for her child undermining her health.

Then had come Borden's murder, this too in another state. The hearing there had unearthed unsavory bits, and that was why the Borden estate had not been settled in Louella's favor.

'Now picture this,' Donna told them. 'Louella finally had to tell her son the truth.

He sought out his true father, Crake. And he was so dismayed he found employment far from his mother and this man who was his father.'

'And this Jim Crake?' Norah asked.

'I don't know,' Donna admitted, 'I understand he had been quite a brilliant young man, had shown great promise in his particular field. Then he had changed.'

She let that sink in and impulsively went on, 'Now that we are being awakened to the realization criminals are but little different from the provably insane, who is to say what occurred within his psyche to change him from unusually brilliant to unusually astute to that other extreme, unusually cunning in achieving his own ends.'

'Murder?' Norah charged.

'A sick mind,' Donna said softly, 'can rationalize. Crake did. The Morgans had somehow destroyed him. Ergo, as they could no longer support him, he would destroy the one who had lured him into their—'

'Lured—' cried Helena, then was suddenly silent, and Donna wondered what button in Helena's motor concept had been touched.

'Well,' the nurse in Donna spoke, 'you have no more reason to worry about rifle fire after or before dark. If you don't mind, I shall take a nap. I was on night duty.'

The chorus came then. 'Will this get into

the newspapers, on the air? Will we ever live it down?'

There was the cry, too, of 'What will my daughter say?' 'Won't my son-in-law make hay of this?'

Donna waited, then held up her hand. Softly she asked, 'Have any one of you thought of your sister Louella, what she has been through these many years? Why not try? If you will excuse me—'

She turned to the tiny cubicle which afforded her only privacy. Slowly the others left the Montel suite, but their voices carried the overtone, 'Oh, the disgrace of it.'

Donna was weary, emotionally fatigued, eager for rest, yet her mind swept back to review the many events, then came finally to Louella's son. He had had the bitterness of learning he did not belong to Borden. He had sought out his father, rejected him and then taken off to another country.

What price the Morgan Manor? she wondered. What had the father of the Morgan girls really left them and their children?

She slept fitfully, awakening at ten to call Dr Haskell and report on the patient's condition. He ordered another check at two and another call so she might delay bringing Mrs Montel in.

Lunch was prepared. She made the two o'clock call after an extra dressing and reported improvement.

'Fine. I'm heading for the coast over the weekend. If the patient continues to improve, we'll wait. I'll swing over that way.'

Mrs Montel was delighted at the news. Nurse must see to it that the Manor was at its best. Such an important person, Dr Haskell.

Another call to another hospital. Mrs Borden was resting well; if she continued to improve she could be returned home within three days.

Donna took time to check on Fanetta and to wonder if she were not in greater need of help than either Mrs Montel or Louella. Phlebetis would respond to medication. A flesh wound would heal. But shattered nerves were so intangible one could neither dress nor ease them, save with tranquilizers, and Fanetta was not the type to ingest those with any security.

'That third game you spoke of,' she asked eagerly, 'will you teach me that one? The earlier ones are helping, yet—'

'Yet you need something more. That is called Goal. You dream up the happiest kind of life you could live in the near future; one without guilt or any negative aspect whatsoever. Picture it in detail; then go over it daily until it becomes a reality. Incidentally, did you finish that painting?'

'Do you mean women of our age can start

anew?'

Norah had overheard and now posed this question.

'Many do,' Donna assured her. 'You read mostly about men, retired, bored, coming alive when they turn their hobbies into careers, or occasionally a different type of business.'

'Hmm,' said Norah, 'I think I shall try that game.'

Comparative peace settled on the Morgan mansion. Days, rain-flooded, passed. Henry spent most of his time in barns and sheds readying machinery for the next step: the planting of crops for another year.

'Forty-three million dollar loss in crops in this seventy-mile valley alone,' he read them from a newspaper, then smiled wryly. 'If misery loves company—'

'I still think something could be done,' intoned Helena.

Stoutly Norah came to Henry's defense. 'Every business has its ups and downs. Helena, remember the year Father said we'd have no Christmas unless we hand-made it?'

'And we had more fun that year than any other I remember,' Fanetta offered.

'Then we'd better start hand-making again,' gloomed Helena.

Louella was returned from the hospital. Possibly because she came by ambulance, the psychological effect was excellent. Three sisters stood at the entrance to greet her, and Mrs Montel, wheeled to her now safe balcony, waved to her from above.

She even, the sisters said the next morning, brought good weather with her.

For suddenly, even as the heavens had poured water over the world, they now made up for lost summer to pour blazing heat.

And the Morgan mansion had an invasion. Sons-in-law, daughters and children of all sizes and description came to vacation.

Donna was confident she would never be able to sort them out, rejoiced they occupied another wing and that she, preparing meals for both Mrs Montel and Louella, need not meet them head on.

And then she identified one man 'having it out,' as he called it, with Henry.

'You need a nurse around here like a horse needs an extra leg. Think of the cost, man. Your Mother Jan is walking now. Louella is out of danger. Yet you pay off money the estate needs to keep a white-starched dead-pan on duty.'

'That white-starched dead-pan,' Henry informed him, 'is one dedicated girl who is now spending a so-called vacation in this madhouse at no cost to the estate. Now maybe you or one of the others would like to keep up the special diets those two sisters are on and dress their wounds?'

'Oh, I didn't understand. Well, she

couldn't find a nicer place to—'

'Sit it out?' asked Henry, stressing the word 'sit.' 'Tom, you'd better clear your eyes or your mind and judge according to realities, not theories.'

Tom. Tom Decker, who'd wanted five thousand from his mother-in-law, Helena Cartwright, to invest in some business he proposed opening.

Henry walked off, but Donna heard Tom's last words. 'Vacation. Not bad. Now when this comes into *my* possession—'

Optimist, Donna said to herself, yet she wondered. Why did he believe Helena, second from the eldest, would outlive the others?

She hadn't found the answer when she noticed Helena Cartwright coming toward her.

'Nurse, I know how busy you are,' she began in an ingratiating tone, 'but could you help me? I have such distress in here.'

She moved her plump hand over such an extensive portion of her anatomy Donna couldn't isolate any area.

'How long since you've had a check-up?'

There came a moment of thought, then a shake of the head. 'Oh, a year or two. You don't think—'

'I think it would relieve your mind if you would arrange for one. Then if you have something organic—'

'Will you take me in?'

Would she? With two daughters, two sons-in-law and a bevy of nephews and nieces able to drive?

'You make the appointment and we'll find someone.'

She spoke to Mrs Montel when she went out to enjoy a bit of late afternoon sea breeze, washing in over the mountains.

'Has your sister always been as healthy as she seems to be now?'

She went into a résumé of childhood illnesses. 'Usually to win some point,' Janice Montel admitted. 'She really swooned when father frowned on Cal Cartwright. I think that was why he gave in to their marriage. He had looked upon him as an opportunist.' Then, at Donna's puzzled expression, 'He believed Cartwright hoped to gain status and probably money from the Manor.

'And she did have a miserable marriage, though she stuck it out. I mean she must have heard what was going on but simply closed her ears. Oh,' she broke off to say, 'why, Nurse, isn't that called—'

'Disassociation from the problem,' Donna agreed. Then she glanced down. 'My word, what is going on down there?'

Mrs Montel gave a crooked smile. 'A family conclave. There was some insistence I join, but I refused. However, I see them wheeling Louella down. Nurse—' she waited a moment—'maybe you'd better go down. Henry is approaching, and I simply do not like the way he's marching, as though he were going into battle.'

Donna looked down at Henry and laughed, 'I'd call it a command performance,' she said.

However, she thought wistfully, there was no one else in the world to whom she would rather have given any support within her power.

The family was really lined up. A long, long wooden bench with long, long board seat attached had been brought in by 'the children' when they arrived for their vacation and demanded cook-outs as part of their fun.

Now this table was lined with family members. Donna, in the shadow of a side entrance, looked at them tabulate their desire to be there or a thousand miles away.

Henry stood facing Tom Decker, and Tom's voice was ringing with authority.

'I realize you've done your best, Emerson, where the Morgan girls and estate are concerned, but, man, face it. You are nothing but a farmer. I am a businessman, and the family has voted unanimously that I be the one to take over immediately. Mother,' exasperation swept in, 'must you—'

Mrs Cartwright, shock on an ashen face, was trying to work her way from the table. In

128

another moment Nurse Donna had cleared the space between them and caught her as she doubled forward.

'Henry, call town, fire department, disaster unit. She needs oxygen.'

CHAPTER ELEVEN

'Call an ambulance.' Decker's voice rose above hers.

'Henry.'

But he was speeding toward the house, even as every person within the area was speeding to the now prone figure of Helena Cartwright.

'Stand back,' snapped Donna. 'She needs every bit of air—'

It was a boy of perhaps fifteen who took over, pushing back parents, cousins, everyone, assuring them the nurse was right.

Yet to Donna the time lapse between Mrs Cartwright's collapse and the first faint call of the siren seemed endless.

Henry returned to report they'd called the nearest hospital for service to dovetail with that of the disaster car.

Later he said Tom Decker had sworn he was trying to assure himself *his* bid to the estate, via his mother-in-law, was canceled; hence he couldn't be trusted.

'Which means,' Donna mused, 'that was what he might have done had it been Mrs Montel. Oh, Henry, this is a house of greed.'

'I know. Man, how I'd like to take Tom up on his dare. I can't. Not right now. If I did it this year it would throw all of "the girls" to the wolves.'

Sons-in-law, daughters and children had fled with the ambulance. Later they called and reluctantly admitted the nurse had been right in her treatment. It had been a coronary; Mrs Cartwright seemed to be pulling out as well as could be expected. They'd stand by, have dinner in town, come home when they were assured 'mother will make it.'

Those remaining were fed, Mrs Montel's slowly healing limbs were dressed, and she was put to bed. After putting on one of her favorite television programs, Donna excused herself for a moment to check on Louella and Fanetta.

They were subdued but vocal. Louella, brighter than before her near tragedy, said perhaps each of the Morgan girls had to face life before she could adjust to it. She intended to as soon as her physician agreed. She was writing her son, clarifying all that had happened in the past. She believed he would forgive her through understanding.

Fanetta, a bit grim, was checking costs. She needed paints, canvases. As yet she did not know how she was going to turn her hobby into anything but part-time relaxation, yet that seemed pretty vital to her right now.

Back in the cool of the balcony, Donna found Henry there, almost relaxed. He did sink down again when assured she was comfortable.

'You know, Hank,' she tried out the name, 'we've all agreed on one thing. Helena's heart attack was precipitated by stress. Now admittedly it had been building up for a long time as she allowed tensions to mount. Then today—'

'Yet she agreed to let Tom say he was superseding me here.'

'Maybe some day you'll have a son-in-law.'

'Like him?' He roared so loudly Mrs Montel called from the inner room and they had to explain his indignation to her.

'But,' Donna continued, 'that was what brought on the extreme tension. Intuitively she knew none could do better than you. Pressured, she agreed to let this Tom—'

'Wait till tomorrow.' He chuckled. 'Look out there; what do you see?'

In the late light the fields looked like tangled and soiled yarn thrown down by a giant.

'Tom's all for letting it reseed itself, saving the cost of seed,' Henry disparaged. 'I couldn't get it across to him that it would reseed and mass up, leaving debris through which it had grown so thick the next crop could not be harvested.'

'And tomorrow?'

Henry pointed to the northeast horizon where a flame, like a dragon, went loping along, leaving sparks and thick smoke behind.

'Tomorrow I start burning.'

'All day? Though I do think I could leave Mrs Montel for an hour or so, don't you? As you know, I'm wearing uniforms mostly because I haven't gone home for replacements. No cap, but I don't want this Tom to make a thing of my being on duty without—'

'I know. I'd like you to take pay, but you're stubborn. This isn't my idea of a vacation for a nurse.'

'That can come later. This—well, it's—oh, call it unfinished business. I can't explain.' Then she sat up. 'I don't need to explain to you. Henry, you have that same inner urge. You have to see this through to a successful conclusion before you can go back to your own life.'

A lean brown hand reached out for hers, shaking it as though some pact had been signed. The brown hand did not relinquish its hold for a moment.

'Some day, Donna,' he began, 'if you can

wait—'

And of course the telephone in Mrs Montel's suite would ring at that precise moment.

It was Tom Decker calling Henry, advising him he would be in mid-morning, noon at the latest, to take over.

'Well,' Henry stretched, 'that takes care of that. Here is where I spend the dark hours lighting up the fields.'

'In short, fight instead of flight,' murmured Donna.

He gave her a sudden smile. 'I am glad you're here as a guest, not a nurse. A nurse could be discharged.' And he was gone.

Donna slept well that night. Mrs Montel's condition was improving to such an extent she could move from bed to wheel chair, even take a few steps. Louella's spirits seemed healing as rapidly as the bullet wound, probably because the great fear she had carried for so long had been safely tucked behind bars. She was now gathering strength to appear against him if necessary.

And Norah was in her element. She was, beyond any doubt, the head of the house, Fanetta being too busy with her 'fool paint dabbling.'

Driving off that morning, a list of purchases on a pad beside her, Donna glanced down. She had ordered a particular painting from Fanetta and in so doing had told her of her own inner agony.

'I need the sight of that mountain forever around,' she confided, 'to teach me what I've been watching others being taught: to face up to problems, either learn to live with them or rationalize to where they are no longer a poison in my life.

'And,' she added, 'a reminder that the sooner we face things, regardless of what, and handle them, the better for others concerned. I should have written Toby when I realized a schoolgirl's infatuation is not enduring love.'

My how the landscape had changed since her last drive to the nearest town. The sun shone bright on thousands of acres of grain. In mourning, she would have said, seeing the vast blackened squares and quadrangles.

Some ranchers had already burned and ploughed, and the new upturned earth seemed awaiting eagerly another chance to prove its worth.

Tom Decker had said he could succeed where Henry couldn't because he, Tom, was a businessman while Henry was only a farmer.

Donna laughed. How little he knew of the modern farmer or rancher. Some of the keenest business brains in the nation were heading the business of providing food for that nation. And no rancher, no matter how limited his scope, could survive without the business acumen pertinent to the sale of his produce.

Donna had a delightful half-hour in the dress shop. She found herself tempted to purchase some shocking items, just for the fun of it, then imagined how far she could have gone protecting either Louella or Helena, had she been so clothed.

Color and weight dictated her final discussion. A canceled date gave her an additional hour in a beauty salon to bring her now shaggy russet curls back into even waves, adroitly shaped to her head.

A stop at the druggist's, where she had a moment alone with Pharmacist Newton as her list was being filled.

She congratulated him on having been the one to pinpoint Jim Crake when the first alarm went out.

He frowned. He'd had to, under the circumstances. He had seen him around, but that evening he was slinking in a new fashion.

'He used to be a fine fellow when we went to school together,' he confided. 'Then later, after he and Louella had broken up, he changed. Started downhill. Times I thought that place poured out some poison that changed a man's or woman's personality.'

Then he smiled. 'Seems it hasn't touched you or Hank. You're both still in there fighting.'

She drove home a little slowly. Home, she thought. Who in these last two generations could or had looked upon that edifice as the place of warmth, security and love the word 'home' should mean?

To those at the Manor it had been a place of retreat but only retreat until, once it came into their possession, they could sell and use the proceeds.

There was no one to greet her. A little puzzled, she hurried in, wondering if some fresh emergency had arisen, then found Norah standing staring down toward the music room.

'Listen to it. Is she out of her mind?' she demanded. 'And Fanetta's in there with her. She helped her downstairs. Should she be?'

'She's only using one hand,' Donna comforted her, then went to the doorway to have two radiant faces peer up at her.

'Nurse, guess what Louella has come up with. She's setting music to individuals.'

'Don't you mean people to—'

'No.' Fanetta spoke, while Louella shook her head until her short curls bounced. 'A new kind of clinic. Nurse, what kind of music does—' she saw Norah hovering— 'well, Norah bring to your ears?'

'Really,' muttered Norah.

'All right, eldest sister.' Louella laughed at her. 'A grim, determined monotone.' And she, insofar as she could, pounded out a steady beat.

'And Sister Helena?' the startled Norah asked.

Swiftly Louella played, then elucidated, 'Fumbling chords that peter out before they are completed.'

'I suppose your music is beauti—'

'Oh, my word, no, Norah. I've the worst tempo of the lot of you. Slinky underneath, taking off into upper scales at the wrong—'

'And Fanetta?'

'She just played me,' Fanetta confessed. 'I sound so broken up there is no harmony, no theme.'

'And how about Nurse here?'

Louella looked at her apologetically. 'A brisk rhythm above a low, sad strain she usually covers with tender melody.'

'Don't you understand?' Fanetta made it a plea. 'There are artists who are brave enough to paint subjects with their strongest but underlying characteristics brought to the surface, even as psychiatrists look to the man under the smooth exterior to determine his true emotions.

'Louella is doing it to music. And believe me, from now on I am going to work to correct that shattered sound entitled Fanetta.'

'Hmmm,' buzzed Norah.

'Thank you,' Donna said softly. 'I shall, for the first time, really try to handle that

137

sadness you found.

'Y'know—' she turned to the others— 'Louella may really have something important here. How few of us see or hear what vibrations we send out to this troubled world. I believe many would prefer harmony, but as they don't realize what they are sending forth, they don't or can't correct it.'

'And when they find out, how can they go about it?' demanded Norah.

'By using the mind in a new way,' Donna replied, 'correctively rather than defensively. Oh, Mrs Montel is calling.'

Going upstairs, her attention seemingly engrossed in the intricately wrought iron palings beside her, Donna took a step further. Louella had played out her feeling toward the Morgan mansion the other day.

Was it the actual dwelling or the reaction of those who had peopled it, such as she?

Odors, she thought. Peculiar how each dwelling had a different one, a composite of the many cleaning, perfuming and living scents that went into a menage.

Mrs Montel was sitting up, debating, she admitted, whether she should or should not try to go downstairs.

'I can walk,' she stated, 'but do I want to walk down into the chaos that will be stirred up when Helena's children and in-laws return? I could become so indignant I'd start to stride, with so much emphasis on my legs—'

'Good girl,' cheered Donna. 'You've recognized a danger. Observe it. And why become embroiled?'

'Because I will not have Henry treated like a—'

'Hold it,' warned Donna. 'Henry is most capable of taking care of himself. With you present, he could be handicapped, you being a Morgan.'

With a deep sigh Mrs Montel sank back. 'Peculiar. I never before realized that. But it's true. And,' she warned, 'win or lose, it is he in whom I believe.'

Donna nodded. 'And meanwhile, which of us ever knows what is winning and what is losing? A point, yes, but the overall? Only time can determine that.'

Questioned, she explained the peculiar music wafting up, now that the doors had again been opened. Mrs Montel was entranced.

'Nurse, I wonder what I sound like,' she mused.

A half-hour yet to lunch; Mrs Montel was thoughtful. Donna went out to the balcony, the far northwest area from where she could look up at the mountain which had so disturbed her that first night.

She had to face this. She had a guilt complex because Toby Petri had lost his life on a mountain like that, farther south. But that had been several years ago.

She had heard the old adage: 'Never cry over spilt milk.' It might be wiser not to carry any of that curdled commodity around with one to splash over on innocent bystanders.

Perhaps it was a matter of maturing. How often she had heard relatives of patients sob, 'Had I known then what I know now, this would never have happened.'

But they hadn't known, nor had she. Wasn't her relationship with the people of the future better because she had been through such an experience?

A spurt of wind flashed across the hilltop. An impetuous wind, she thought, then smiled. Toby had been an impetuous man. His friends called him, 'Mister go off before the gun fires.' Perhaps it was this trait which had spurred him into hiring a plane, rather than his immediate need to meet her.

Standing, she shrugged her shoulders. She had carried that burden long enough.

Louella was coming from the hall door. Fanetta was with her, and so was Norah.

What, they demanded of her, should they do about Tom Decker? They had agreed to let him try running the ranch as much for Henry's sake as his own, but now they wondered.

'Why not put Mr Decker to music?' Donna asked Louella. 'And you, Fanetta, make a swift sketch of your reaction to him.'

140

'And me?' asked Norah.

Donna laughed. 'If you have some soft soap, you might try doing a head and shoulders of him. Frankly, I don't know him or the problems, so to work.'

They started to turn, then heard a car and as one swept to the portico.

The family had returned from the hospital.

'But,' stated Decker heavily, 'despite her improvement, those fool doctors wouldn't let me in to have her sign this paper. Oh, you know,' he said irritably, 'her opinion of Hank and her desire to have me installed as top man.'

Donna merely shook her head and walked away. Didn't the man know it was Helena being forced to this action against her better judgment which had precipitated the attack? Yet how many, or rather, how few traced such steps to culmination?

Another car was wending its way along the narrow roadway leading from the county road. More trouble, she wondered idly, or merely the estate executor who was coming in to act as judiciary?

She eased away from the road proper, planning her tomorrow. She would take Louella to one hospital for a check-up, then Mrs Montel to another city and to her own hospital for another. Or would that be necessary?

Swiftly she sped back. That was Dr

Haskell in the car, three women in the rear seat, a young girl beside him.

Donna greeted the doctor happily, accepted introductions to the two women beside his wife, then looked puzzled as he stepped out of the car, went around to let the little girl out and pushed her toward Donna.

She was a pretty child of say six or seven, who faintly reminded her of someone. She had blonde hair, black eyes that slanted a little and a lovely smile.

'Patricia Petri,' Dr Haskell introduced her.

'Papa Toby said if we were ever in trouble to come to you,' the child said earnestly. 'We weren't until Mama got herself TB and we used all his insurance money.'

Haskell, aware of the shock on Donna's face, stepped in quickly. 'You didn't know about this?'

Know that Toby had been married, obviously soon after he had left her to go into service?

She glanced at that particular mountain, sharp and clear against the sky. To think she had carried this heavy burden of guilt all of these years when it had been in part Toby's. He had been afraid even to bring his wife and child to the States until he had cleared the way; obviously afraid even to admit their existence.

No wonder he had defied mountains and storms.

CHAPTER TWELVE

A small voice said, 'See, she doesn't want me, either,' and Donna forgot herself.

With a swift gesture she swooped down, gathered the little girl into her arms and lifted her. 'But I do, dear. I was just so—'

'Shooken?' suggested Patricia.

'Excellent word. Doctor?'

He nodded, satisfied. He had had Donna's background from nurses with whom she had served during the period of Toby Petri's fatal crash on the mountain; knew the guilt she had carried and, when this child had been sent him by the Migrant Labor Camp, believed a swift challenge could more quickly clear Nurse Donna's mind than any long-drawn-out consultation.

'You slip back in the car while the doctor and our nurse here check on her patient. Right?'

Obediently the little girl nodded, returned for a taut hug of Donna's waist, then ran to the car.

Dr Haskell drew Donna into a quiet nook. 'This hasn't been too great a shock, Nurse?'

'Relief, Doctor. I've carried such a burden of guilt. I knew soon after Toby went overseas that I didn't and had never loved him. But I felt that wasn't the time to tell him. When he didn't come home on leave, he said he was "putting away pennies;" no more. Then I felt more guilt than ever.

'I'm afraid I might have married him to ease my own conscience if—'

'About the child: she was aware of you early. After a bitter, destructive raid, her father wrote your name down for her to keep. She was to have the embassy contact you.

'Instead, Petri had both mother and child brought to the States. They arrived just after he headed north. And who knows what plan he had in mind then?

'But about her care: that is not necessary. What she needs currently is the assurance someone who "knew papa Toby" loves her. If you can give that, nothing more need be offered.

'And now shall we check Mrs Montel?'

Haskell gave his findings bluntly. If Mrs Montel lived elsewhere, he would say she was ready to resume normal living, naturally within certain restrictions. But here, with those stairs—

They compromised by arranging for Henry Emerson to wheel her down for the day, after breakfast, and up before dinner. She would lunch downstairs. Perhaps next week she could remain below stairs longer.

Donna was relieved she need not sit out the dinner hour with the entire family.

Henry, she observed, dined elsewhere, though Tom was awaiting him, ready to tell him exactly what he thought of the burning.

At least it was a mile from the Manor.

The next day, driving Louella to the hospital for her check-up, Donna felt as though she were moving into freedom.

Queried by Louella, she said, 'We hear "judge no man," but too often we don't apply that to ourselves. I've been sitting in judgment on myself, in a wrong judgment, for years, doing more harm to others than I realized.'

'I know.' Louella spoke softly. 'I couldn't be completely honest with myself or Jim or Borden, lest it reflect upon my son. I should have fought for the annulment, then let Borden adopt him. Why must we learn things only through suffering?'

'Perhaps, until we suffer, we feel we have all of the answers.'

'Perhaps then,' mused Louella, 'honesty in all avenues is the safest policy.'

Dr Michael gave a thorough test to the incoming Louella, and they had to wait some time before the results were run through the laboratory, yet both seemed to enjoy the change. Donna felt they enjoyed getting away from that house seething with hate.

Michael pronounced Mrs Louella Borden in better condition than when she had first been admitted. This, though, thought

145

Donna, turning her car back west, means that I can now leave Morgan Manor, my part in any reclamation completed.

She mentioned this to Louella, who promptly cried, 'Why don't we celebrate, go to the coast for a day? Maybe even Henry would join us. I know Fanetta wants to.'

Henry would join them. He met them with lips twisted wryly. That day he had received a court summons. He was to show cause why he should not be removed from the Morgan Manor managership. The complaint was signed—well, he hadn't looked farther than Decker's name.

'And we'll take Mother Jan,' he said, 'and all of us go in the station wagon. That I own, personally. Agreed? You—' he faced Louella and Fanetta, who had joined them—'may want to stay. Those here are having a family get-together picnic. Everyone even remotely connected with the Morgans will be on hand to feast in the grove.'

'How early can we leave?' asked Fanetta, and Louella joined in.

Donna waited a moment. Perhaps out of such an affair some union could be reached. But could it be, with Decker in charge?

They set the time. Then Donna murmured to Henry that, as she would be leaving the Morgans on the morrow, she would drive off early, leaving her car at the Newton Pharmacy parking lot.

'Good,' he agreed. 'Not your going exactly, Donna, but who knows how long I shall be there?' Then added, 'Yet how can I walk off and leave her to that—'

House of Hate? Donna finished the thought for him, looking up at the vast edifice now shimmering in the late afternoon sun.

'Pick you up at Newton's at, say, nine o'clock too early? Fine; then off to a new life, we two together.'

There was no time for more. Laughing and screaming children rushed through the portico, and Donna fled to the entrance.

House of Hate? Those voices just below. 'Well, if you ask me, that nurse they brought in has caused most of the distress we've seen. I've been checking on her. When I have enough factual material, I am going to see that she is thrown out of her profession.'

Slowly then she mounted the stairway, looking for the last time on the beauties that lined it, that lay below. She glimpsed wide doorways revealing the rich, irreplaceable furnishings, paintings, tapestries. That chandelier—would any other, could any other be built with as exquisite lines, each curve a story?

As Henry had suggested, she gave Mrs Montel her choice of the two affairs scheduled for the next day. She worried the thought. She supposed she should be here;

one of the Morgan girls, y'know. Yet how she longed for a day at the coast for relaxation, for being with those who neither condemned nor criticized.

Dutifully Donna placed such dressings as she would, after the morning, be using herself, within easy access. She wrote a routine and then sat by, smiling, as Mrs Montel tried to express her gratitude.

During their final meal together on the balcony, Donna was still automatically testing the railings.

They spent a quiet evening despite the noise below, the patient asking what the nurse intended to do about the child who had been literally 'left to' her.

'Love her,' Donna replied; 'see that she has the little extras that mean so much to a child. Check on her mother and when she is released, if I can, help her to establish herself.'

Relaxed, they continued to sit on the balcony. 'It is beautiful here,' Donna murmured, looking out across hundreds of acres to sky-high mountains, dull blue at this hour. One far to the east caught the final rays of the sun, shining white with snow.

'It is really, Nurse?' Mrs Montel spoke heavily. 'Somehow I feel beauty is more than what the eye registers. Our comparatively modest coast home, with no more of a view than a neighbor's house and driveway, seems more beautiful to me than this grandeur.'

Donna sat up alertly. 'You mean you wouldn't mind living elsewhere if—'

'My dear, I only moved here because Henry was in the service and I could not bear being a burden on him when he was released.'

No, she hadn't ever really told him how she felt about this house. There'd been so little happiness in it; so much grief and, of late, so much hatred. At times she wondered if it were worth remaining alive if life had to be spent there.

'To bed with you.' Donna's voice was gay. 'There are new days coming, I promise. And tomorrow we arise at six.'

She was up at six. At six-thirty she dutifully spread a tray on her erstwhile patient's lap, the main component smooth cooked meal with a dab of butter and honey, fresh coffee and one sliver of toast. 'So you'll be ready for lunch.'

At seven-thirty she was leaving the House of Hate when a white-faced Norah Morgan Norton stopped her.

'Why wasn't I invited to the picnic at the coast?' she demanded.

'I assume because it was thought you were presiding at the one here.'

'Naturally, as I am the eldest Morgan girl.'

Donna waited a moment, then, catching sight of her curved hands, murmured, 'Stop

149

being so rigidly right; so ready to accept the concepts of another era, you feel iron-bound—' she let that thought sink in—'to carry them through.'

'You will come back?' There was a wistful quality to the voice.

Donna glanced around at the material beauty, then at the woman who could still have been beautiful had she not been so restricted by the dictates of her father. 'I would rather not,' she admitted frankly, 'but if you ever need me, Mrs Norton, perhaps—'

Newton was opening the pharmacy when Donna drove in. Happily he smiled at her. 'I'd like to know your chemical component,' he told her. 'You've made a new man of Henry, turned him from a beaten drudge to a free ranging man of adventure. He tells me others in that—'

'House of Hate?' she asked.

'That you've freed them, too. How did you do it?'

'I didn't,' she said softly, 'I too was bound by false evaluations. And I am now also free.'

He made one other remark which sent Donna toward the corner where the station wagon should be waiting, her cheeks pink.

Henry was there, as were the other three: Mother Jan, Fanetta, Louella. Happily he ushered her into the seat beside him, and they set forth.

Perhaps there are days destined to bring

natural beauty to its peak. It was not really autumn, yet the vine maple stood out scarlet on the banks, touched other trees with the first dabs of gold, intensified the stark green of conifers and turned the overhead sky to a startling azure.

And Henry knew his coast. He knew which turn would take them to access to a sheltered cove. Tenderly he helped Mother Jan down a slightly precipitous path, spread a blanket and settled her down, then returned for Louella and Fanetta and finally for Donna.

'You don't seem worried about that court summons,' she charged, as he brought baskets of food from the rear of the wagon.

'Funny thing.' He stopped, arms laden. 'I felt it was a reprieve; more than that, as though someone had turned the key to a cell into which I had been pushed and held and from which I couldn't free myself. Now, do you think I am crazy?'

'No.' She shook her head. 'You don't personalize, blame any individual. You sense it was the House of Hate in action. Oh, come on, quick—'

'Donna—' he caught at her with a half free hand—'you know what this means. Or do you? I don't want to go back. I'm even half convinced I'll be harming the Morgan girls if I do. Perhaps they can't face reality until it faces them.

'And meanwhile I have no job. I could almost say I've hardly a dime left, I've poured so much into that—'

'Wonderful,' she cheered.

'Wonderful? But, Donna, that means I can't ask you to marry me.'

'Why not? Does one have to have a manor house filled with the past; or have a job, position, what have you, handled under duress? Henry—' they had passed through a cleft of mossy rock to the shore—'I'd really rather take my chances pitching a tent on that and letting fresh air, fresh happiness, fresh love sweep in—And do not drop that basket; come on!'

'A wonderful day,' they all breathed contentedly, heading back to the inner valley after sunset.

It had been. Fanetta had hovered over a canvas, Louella had made small murmurings and drawn scale notes on chance bits of paper. Mrs Montel had apparently dwelt on happy memories.

Yet a certain sadness seemed to settle on them as they drove through a famous corridor reserved for wild life, protected from man's destruction of native trees.

They sped along small rivers which seemed to dwindle as the road mounted and then came out eventually to valleys.

Tonight, Donna thought, she would be back in her apartment looking down on city lights. But these others would be back in the House of Hate, looking out on—

'Oh, no!' screamed one of the three in the rear. 'Henry, the Manor! Look! Look there to the southeast!'

They looked to the southeast where normally there would have stood a mansion. Now there was only a black pall of smoke.

Mrs Montel spoke defiantly. 'It couldn't!'

'It has!' Henry returned as they swung onto the home road to find rural fire equipment from many districts lining it.

Oh, true, there were upthrusts of defiance where metal had refused to cower to heat, but the house *per se* had vanished, collapsed into masses of ash and debris.

'Stay in the car,' Henry ordered the older women, then with Donna sped forward to where a group of men stood about a boy, the defiant center of a circle.

'All right; I'll tell you.' He spoke in a sharp, thin voice. 'All that place ever meant to our family was a pot to brew up poison. It ruined the life of anyone who lived in or around it.

'Take Dad. Until he married into it he was a regular guy. Now look at him. No job was good enough because Mom was going to benefit from this some day—this poison pot. She and Dad were going to see grandma outlive the rest of them.

'Okay. That's the way it went with all of

them. I used to play-pretend I was wrecking it with a bomb or something when we had to live here. I didn't try because there were always old women around.

'Today there weren't any old women. Grandma was in the hospital, Mother's Aunt Norah down beyond the brush where we were going to have a picnic, the rest of them at the coast.

'So put me in jail if you want to. I did what I'd been planning to do for a long, long time, and I'm not sorry.'

He had made careful preparation, hoarding inflammable material, then watching for the precise moment when he could strew it to ignite such things as drapes, divans—anything that would catch quickly.

This day none of the 'old ladies' had been around, so with the rest of the crowd sitting down to their barbecue, all closed off from the Manor by that tall brush, he'd started the fire.

The fire was so far under way before smoke had burst from its cloistered interior, that there had been no chance even to reach a telephone. Tom had had to race to the nearest farm to call for help.

Oil tanks, recently filled for initial winter use, though set some distance from the house, had undergone combustion, even as the bomb the boy had planned would some day destroy the building.

A deputy sheriff pushed his hat back, puzzled. He had sons of his own. He knew boys. Here was no bravado, no evasion, just a simple statement of facts.

'Why are you making this confession?' he demanded.

For the first time Tom Decker's son looked down, seemingly engrossed in soot-smudged sandals.

'I didn't mean to,' he admitted. 'I sort of figured maybe there'd be some other reason could be given. And then I heard the folks. Man, everybody was blaming everybody else, aiming to get even, sue them, have them slashed off the will.

'It was vicious. It was the pouring out of more poison than I'd ever heard before. I figured if I told the truth, the other folks wouldn't get blamed, and we wouldn't have to go through days and weeks, maybe years, of living it over.'

Under questioning he elucidated further, and Donna began to wonder if this much maligned generation was not more realistic than her own and the senior Morgans'.

Henry touched her arm. They returned to the station wagon, where Norah had joined the others.

Henry briefed them, then listened to the wails, each an echo of the others. All of their wordly goods were gone, all of their momentos.

'Those you have in your mind,' he told them. 'You must have or you wouldn't remember them. Not one of you has seen any of them since you moved to the Morgan mansion. They were always packed, always stowed away awaiting the day *you* would inherit the place.'

'But what are we going to do?' came the chorus.

'Oh, that. This being Sunday, you may have to borrow my pajamas. But, Mother Jan, the reason I have personally been skimping on cash is this. I bought back our old home—yes, dear, the one you loved and gave up. It's been rented each summer, furnished. Might not have done too good a job on that, but you can all make-do for a while, can't you?

'Utilities are on, so suppose we pile back into the wagon and go down to the Montels'. Donna, you're part of our family, aren't you?'

Donna glanced up through the smoke haze to a mountain peak which seemed to have shrunk.

'Definitely,' she caroled. 'So much a part I'll take Norah with me, and we'll stop to shop for breakfast.'

'We haven't had dinner yet.'

'That we can buy at a take-out. You do have dishes down there, Henry?'

They started west again, Henry's wagon

making better speed than Donna's small car. This stopped at a market near Newton's where they loaded up with 'possibilities,' as Donna called them.

Traveling on, she glanced at Norah. Norah sat relaxed, her hands limp.

'I don't have to fight to hold things together any more,' Norah stated in wonderment, laughed a little and said there was nothing left to hold. And she was glad. She hoped the others felt the same way.

She would like to be the one to tell Helena; tell her she need no longer 'brace against anything.'

And of course, none of them needed really to worry about the future. As the eldest, she knew the will by heart. It held only as long as Morgan Manor stood.

Donna looked at her in shock.

'Yes, now the land can be sold.' And no, that information had been given only to the eldest living member of the family. However, as there was no longer a house, her lips were no longer sealed.

The land could be sold, the proceeds evenly divided! Five sisters who had sat out years of poisonous hate were now free to begin a new life, free of each other, if they so desired; free at least of the shadows of the House of Hate.

They drove through a vast flock of southbound starlings, hundreds of them

157

polka-dotting the sky. The Morgans had been driving through thoughts as swift and dark for years.

The Montel cottage was comparatively modest. With fog sweeping in from the sea which lay beyond a low range of hills, the warmth was most welcome.

They had dinner before a hearth blazing with driftwood; then wearily the sisters went to the appointed areas where they would sleep. There was a den for Donna and a divan for Henry.

Yet they sat on watching the embers.

Donna silenced him once. 'Henry, what price a manor or vast fields of potential gain? If we start together with love instead of hate, we won't need material things.'

'With you, Donna Maria, I need nothing more.'